The

Inheritance

by Carol Hall

Cover art by Aiden Short

This book is dedicated to Carla, Kristyn and Joshua who know of my love of ghost stories.

Chapter 1

Carly Montgomery sat across the large mahogany desk from Mr. Bloomfield, Attorney at Law. She stared dumbly at him for several moments before he cleared his throat and raised his eyebrows. "Do you understand what I just told you?" he asked her.

"Um, I think so," she replied, scanning the document that lay on the desk in front of her.

"You do understand that you now own Montgomery Manor? That you are the sole heir to Miss Ruth Montgomery?"

"Yes, but..," Carly began. "Why me?"

Mr. Bloomfield shuffled a stack of papers and pulled one out to examine it.

"It says here that you are her only living relative."

"How can that be? I've never heard of her before," Carly said. She pushed the paper back across the table towards him. "I never knew I had an aunt."

Mr. Bloomfield scratched the side of his head and flipped through the stack of papers again. He slid the one she had handed back to him into the stack before speaking.

"Miss Montgomery had been a client of mine for many years. Truth be told, I didn't realize she had any family either. She never spoke of any of them, or you. It wasn't until she had me draw up this Last Will and Testament for her that I even knew of your existence."

Carly sat there dumbfounded. An aunt. She had an aunt. Her father had never mentioned her. Since his passing four years ago, and her mother having passed at her birth, she had thought she was alone in the world.

"My aunt never married?" she asked. "I noticed that her last name was still Montgomery." The hope that maybe she had cousins out there somewhere, brought a slight spark of hope to her.

"No, she never married," Mr. Bloomfield said. "Oh, there were rumors of a beau when she was young, but if that was true or not, only Ruth knew."

Carly let out a long sigh. Oh well, no cousins after all.

At twenty seven years old, and being an only child, she had spent the last two years on her own. When her father died, he had left her the house they had lived in and a small amount of cash, but the money didn't last long and she eventually sold the house and moved into an apartment in town.

"I was given strict instructions to pass on to you before you can claim the house and property," said Mr. Bloomfield.

Carly's mind snapped back to the subject at hand and she nodded at him. "Ok."

"First of all," he said. "You are not to sell the property. Miss Ruth insisted on this. She states that in order for you to inherit everything, you must agree to move into and reside in the house."

Carly's mouth fell open. "What? But why? That means I'll have to quit my job and move all the way down here."

"She was adamant about this," Mr. Bloomfield said. "The property has been in your family since the 1800s and she insisted you must live in it to inherit it. I don't begin to understand her reasons, but I am required to inform you of her wishes."

Carly nodded and waved her hand at him, implying for him to continue.

"Secondly, you must maintain the house and grounds. You are not permitted to allow the property to fall into disrepair."

Again, Carly nodded and allowed him to continue.

"Thirdly, you are to keep in your employment, a one Mr. Vernon Knowles. He is the groundskeeper. He is to be permitted to continue living in the carriage house, rent free, for as long as he chooses to stay. And he is to be paid the first of every month in the amount specified in the Will."

"So...I'm required to keep and pay for a groundskeeper, maintain the property and attend to any and all repairs the place may need," Carly clarified. "And just how am I supposed to do all that on a school teacher's salary?"

"Miss Ruth has left you a sizable amount of money to go along with the property," Mr. Bloomfield said. He shuffled through the paperwork again and pulled out a sheet of paper and laid it on the table in front of her. "I think this should see you through for quite some time."

Carly looked at the number written on the document and gasped. "Are you serious?" she asked, looking at Mr. Bloomfield. "This isn't a typo?"

Mr. Bloomfield pulled the paper back toward himself and examined the number written on it. "I assure you, it is correct."

"Is there anything else I should know?" Carly asked, still unable to process everything she had learned thus far.

"No, I think that about does it, Miss Montgomery. Once you sign this form agreeing to Miss Ruth's terms, it's all yours."

Carly scribbled her name on the document and passed it back to Mr. Bloomfield.

"Well, congratulations, Miss Montgomery. You are now the proud owner of Montgomery Manor. Here are the keys," he said, dropping them into her hand. "I wish you all the best."

"Thank you, sir," Carly said, wrapping her fingers around the set of keys. "I really appreciate all your help."

Rising from her chair, she shook Mr. Bloomfield's hand and turned to go.

"Don't forget your paperwork," Mr. Bloomfield called to her. "You'll need it when you go set things up with the bank and deed office."

She reached out and took the envelope from him that contained the Will and slid it into her large handbag. "Thanks again, sir," she said.

"Oh, and Miss Montgomery," he said, lowering his voice slightly. "Don't let the townsfolk scare you with all the talk about ghosts. People just love to tell tall tales."

Carly just stared at him with her mouth open and slowly nodded. "Right…," she said, as she turned and walked out the door.

Chapter 2

Carly spent the next week cleaning out her apartment and saying goodbye to her friends.

Since she was moving into her aunt's already furnished house, she wouldn't need any of her own furniture or household items, so she gave as much of it as she could to her friends and neighbors and donated the rest to a local charity.

School was not in session since it was mid June, so she didn't have an opportunity to say goodbye to her students. Instead, she sent emails to each of the parents explaining the situation and asking them to pass her love and hugs on to the kids.

Her fellow teachers had thrown her a going away party. Since it was on such short notice, there wasn't much time to prepare anything extravagant, so they hosted a simple affair in the town's small city park and sent her on her way with lots of tears, hugs, and well wishes. She knew she would miss them and promised to email each one of them once she got settled.

As she loaded the few personal items she was taking with her into the trunk of her car, she couldn't help but wonder what her new home would be like.

She had been unprepared for the call from the lawyer explaining to her that she was to come to his office at her earliest convenience to go over her aunt's Will. An aunt she didn't even know she had.

After learning she was to inherit her estranged aunt's property, along with a large sum of money, she didn't know what to do. When she left the attorney's office, instead of going to her newly acquired home, she panicked and headed straight back to her apartment in the small town she grew up in to gather her thoughts and figure out what her next move was going to be.

Now, as she slid behind the wheel of her car and prepared to head to her new home, apprehension filled her. She had never lived anywhere but the small town she was now leaving. She wouldn't know anyone. Would she be able to make new friends? She would have to find a job teaching somewhere. Was there a school close by? She realized she didn't know anything about her new home.

She supposed she could have pulled out the paperwork from the envelope that contained the Last Will and Testament and learned a little bit about it, but nerves made her keep it sealed shut and stuffed deep down in the bottom of her suitcase.

What was she was so afraid of anyway? She had been on her own for a few years now, so it couldn't be that. Was it the fear of a new town? Of not knowing anyone? No, she didn't think that was it either.

If she was honest with herself, she knew why she was a bit apprehensive about going.

The words Mr. Bloomfield had said to her as she was walking out of his office had rung in her ears for days. *Don't let the townsfolk scare you with all the talk about ghosts.* Why would the townsfolk think the place was haunted? And worse yet, was it?

Carly shook her head to clear away those thoughts. "Oh, stop being ridiculous," she told herself out loud. "There's no such thing as ghosts."

She glanced down at a small piece of paper laying on the seat next to her. The address for Montgomery Manor stared back at her in bold, black ink. 18 Oak Grove Rd. *Well,* she thought, *it has a nice ring to it, at least.*

She pulled out of the apartment complex and headed south.

The five hour drive gave her plenty of time to think. Had she made the right move giving up her job and apartment and moving to an unfamiliar place? The attorney had said that it had gardens and a carriage house. How big was the property? She could slap herself now for not looking at the deed to see just exactly what it was she had inherited. For all she knew, it could be a run down dump in the middle of nowhere. But she couldn't forget the sizable amount of money that came with the property. It couldn't be all that bad if her aunt had that kind of money, could it?

What about neighbors? Would they all be old like her aunt? What was the town like? Would she fit in with the community or be considered an outsider?

Her head was swimming with tons of questions, but no answers.

She cranked up the radio and stepped on the gas. "May as well get there and see for myself," she said out loud to herself.

~~~

The drive seemed excruciatingly long. Carly stopped for lunch half way through the trip, but realized her stomach was in knots and the hamburger she bought only made her nauseated. Tossing it in the trash, she opted for her bottle of water and a small granola bar that she had thrown into her purse instead.

By mid afternoon, her GPS alerted her that she was getting close to her destination. Within half an hour, she would arrive at her new home.

She turned off the highway and after passing through a small town, began to follow a windy, dirt road for several miles.

The houses thinned out and eventually they were spaced a considerable distance apart.

Spanish moss hung from the trees overhead creating a tunnel effect on the road. Through small openings in the canopy, rays of sunlight dotted the scenery.

Carly soaked in the beauty around her. *It truly is beautiful here*, she thought to herself as she surveyed her surroundings. Through the trees on either side of the road, she could see large fields full of tall grass and summertime flowers.

The dirt road continued on for several more miles before her GPS squawked out it's directions. "*Turn left in half a mile.*"

Carly sat up straight in her seat and looked intently out the front windshield. A black wrought iron fence came into view. It ran along the stretch of road leading up to the driveway.

"*You have reached your destination*," the GPS voice informed her.

Turning her blinker on, she made a left hand turn onto a long, curvy, graveled road that was lined with tall, thickly leafed trees on both sides. Two stone pillars marked the end of the driveway. A mailbox was situated into the side of one of the pillars. The number 18 was etched into the stone above the box.

"This must be it," Carly said, taking a deep breath and blowing it out between pursed lips.

She wound her way up the long drive until it opened up to reveal a circular parking area surrounded by lush flower beds. In the center of the drive was a large flowerbed circled by stones with a tall water fountain in the middle of it.

Carly's mouth dropped open at the huge, two story, white mansion that rose impressively before her eyes. Four tall, white pillars ran the length of the large front porch, reaching up to the second story. The porch wrapped around the house until it disappeared out of sight around both sides. Several tall windows graced the front of the house, flanked on the sides by black shutters. It was the most beautiful house Carly had ever seen.

She couldn't take her eyes off the house as she slowly eased herself out of the car. She tore her eyes away just long enough to reach inside and grab the little slip of paper that had the address scribbled on it. She read the address out loud and looked back up at the house again. "This can't be right," she said, shaking her head.

"Who are you?" came a gruff male voice from the side of the house.

Carly snapped her head in the direction of the sound. An old man, slightly bent over, with a mop of short gray hair came hobbling over toward her. "I asked who you are," he demanded. "If you're selling something, we ain't interested."

"Oh, I'm sorry, sir," Carly stammered. "I'm not selling anything. I'm Carly. Carly Montgomery. I was Ruth Montgomery's niece."

The old man wrinkled up his nose as if he smelled something bad and mumbled something under his breath.

"Excuse me?" Carly asked. "I didn't catch that."

"Nevermind," he said between clenched teeth. "So you're the new owner of this place, huh?"

"Yes, sir," Carly said, approaching him with her hand held out. "It appears so. You must be Vernon Knowles, correct?"

Ignoring her hand, he simply nodded.

Carly dropped her hand to her side and cleared her throat. "Well, don't worry, Vernon. I'm not going to kick you out or ask you to leave. You're more than welcome to stay and continue to care for the grounds and property as you always have."

"You're darn right I am, missy," he said, his voice rising. "You can't kick me out or ask me to leave. I know what Miss Ruth put in her Will. I'm to stay as long as I want and…," he pointed at her chest. "You have to keep paying me."

"Yes, sir," Carly said, a little affronted. "You're right. And I fully intend on fulfilling that agreement."

"Like you have a choice," Vernon mumbled under his breath.

Carly was flabbergasted as she watched Vernon turn on his heel and walk off without so much as a word of goodbye.

She grabbed her handbag and suitcase out of the car and climbed the three steps up onto the veranda. Fishing the keys out of her pocket, she inserted the proper one into the keyhole and swung the door open.

She gasped as she took in the sight before her. A large, curved staircase wound its way up to the second floor. A crystal chandelier hung in the center of the ceiling casting little prisms of light around the room. Old oil paintings of country settings adorned the walls on each side of the foyer area. A large intricately woven area rug was laid out in the center of the floor. Off to the left was a large sitting room with a fireplace visible from the foyer and to the right was an office with a large mahogany desk sitting under a large floor to ceiling window.

Carly dropped her bags where she stood and slowly spun around in a circle, taking note of everything she could see. The house was massive. She looked past the grand staircase and saw a kitchen at the back of the house.

She picked up her bags and walked down the hall toward the kitchen. It was painted in a light cheery yellow with up-to-date stainless steel appliances. Carly determined she was going to love this room. A faint smell of lemon hung in the air and the soft whoosh, whoosh of the ceiling fan made the room feel clean and airy.

Laying her handbag down on the island counter, she turned and headed back down the hall toward the stairs, grabbing her suitcase as she went. She couldn't wait to check out the upstairs and see where the master bedroom was.

As she sprinted up the wide, carpeted stairs, she let out a little giggle. She felt like a kid at Christmas. This couldn't be possible, could it? She really owned this place? It was like a dream come true.

She got to the top of the stairs and couldn't decide whether to go to the left first or to the right, so she opted to go left. Walking down the long hallway, she noticed four doors which must lead to four bedrooms. She opened the first door and sure enough, it was a bedroom done in soft pastel colors. She opened the next door and it also opened up into a bedroom, this one done in deep blues and purples.

She proceeded to open each door and each door opened up into a bedroom, with each room being done in different colors.

She retraced her steps back to the stairs and followed the hallway down to the right. This end of the hall only had three doors. Two along the hallway and one at the very end. Opening the two doors along the hallway, she discovered, they too, were bedrooms.

When she got to the door at the end of the hall, she hesitated before opening it. The heavy, dark stained, wooden door seemed almost imposing. She noticed the black, old fashioned door knob and lock. Turning it gently in her hand, the latch clicked and the door slowly opened a few inches. Carly gingerly pushed the door until it opened all the way to reveal the most opulent room she had ever seen.

A huge four-poster bed made out of dark wood was set against the far wall. Long, heavy drapes in a deep maroon and gold trim hung from the canopy and gave the bed an almost cave like appearance. Matching drapes hung from the tall windows on either side of the bed. Two dark wood dressers were set on each side of the room and a massive armoire was placed on the wall next to the door. The room had hardwood floors with a large, thick area rug laid out in the center.

The room was dark and gloomy, but Carly didn't care. That could be changed with a little paint and a new bedspread.

She threw her suitcase on the bed and began to unpack her belongings, shoving them into the dressers and armoire.

Looking around she noticed a door off to the right of the bed. Opening it up she discovered the bathroom. She was a bit disappointed in it's grandeur, or rather, lack thereof. The whole house was so rich in character and furnishings, but the master bathroom was rather plain and unimpressive. A simple white porcelain sink was placed under a simple square mirror. The white and green checkered tile floor was old looking and ugly. A claw foot tub was up against the far wall under a frosted window. The toilet was behind a small door at the end of the tub.

"Oh well," Carly said, laying out her toothbrush and cosmetics. "I guess it'll have to do."

She laughed at herself for such a snooty comment. She was used to the simpler things in life, so this bathroom was just what she was accustomed to. But still, she had to admit, it was a bit cold and impersonal.

"Nothing a little paint won't fix," she said out loud. "And maybe some new curtains and colorful rugs."

She finished getting herself settled in and headed back down the stairs to finish checking out her new home.

The house was furnished with what Carly assumed were antiques. The furnishings had an oldtimey feel to them and the paintings were all of outdoor, country themes. Large lamps with painted globe bases sat on old side tables and odd knickknacks of various kinds of birds and figurines were set about the place.

As Carly explored her new home, she realized, that while it was a very well kept, beautiful home, there were several things she would be getting rid of, as well as updating some of the furniture and fixtures. Now that she owned the house, she wanted to put her own personal touches to it.

She stepped outside onto the veranda and took in the vastness of the grounds. Flowerbeds were spread out in all directions. Gravel paths with solar lights wound their way through the property. A garden gate to the left of the house led into a large rose garden ensconced by a four foot high stone wall. The sweet smell of the roses filled the air. Inhaling a deep breath of the pleasant smell, Carly headed off toward the other side of the house.

As she rounded the corner, the carriage house came into view. It was a large, two story structure set back away from the house at the rear. Off to the side of it was the garden shed, where Carly assumed Vernon kept all the lawn equipment.

She wandered on past the carriage house and climbed a small embankment. There, she saw a small cemetery perched on top of the hill, set a ways back from the house. Beyond the cemetery, was a shallow river. She could hear the gurgling, bubbly water rushing over the rocks.

She walked through the cemetery looking at the names on each of the gravestones. These must have been her ancestors. Mr. Bloomfield had told her that this property had been in her family since before the Civil War. A feeling of connection, of belonging, came over her as she walked among the graves and saw the history of the family that she never knew, buried here.

She noticed one of the headstones was much larger and broader at the base then the rest of them. Walking over to it, she read the inscription. *Here lies Rutherford H. Montgomery, Sept. 1801 – July 1869, May he rest in peace.*

Carly stared at the inscription for a few moments. "I wonder if Aunt Ruth was named after him?" she asked out loud.

"Yes, she was," came a voice from behind her.

She gasped loudly and swung around. A man was approaching her from the direction of the river.

"I didn't mean to startle you," he told her. His voice was deep, with a rich tone to it.

Carly watched the man approach her before saying anything. "Who are you and where did you come from?"

The man chuckled deep in his throat and stepped up to her, holding out his hand.

"I'm Joe Fortner," he said, as he shook her hand. "I'm your closest neighbor. "I've been keeping an eye on the place ever since Ruth passed away. I heard there was a new owner and I was just on my way over to the house to meet you when I saw you come up the hill toward the cemetery."

"It's nice to meet you, Joe. I'm Carly. Carly Montgomery."

"So you are," Joe said, giving her a once over.

Carly couldn't help but stare back at Joe. He was tall, maybe six foot three with dark, wavy hair that was tucked behind his ears and the bluest eyes she had ever seen. So blue, in fact, that they almost appeared translucent.

"So…," Joe said. "What are your plans for the place?"

"P..p..plans?" Carly was embarrassed that she stuttered the word. She was so busy taking in his broad shoulders and muscular physique that she wasn't prepared for the question.

"Yeah, what do you intend to do with the place?"

Carly gained her composure and quickly brushed a strand of her hair behind her ear. She gazed up into his face and nearly fainted. *Oh my,* she thought, *get yourself together. You've seen good looking men before.*

"I'm not sure exactly," she said. She realized she was fiddling with her hands and quickly dropped them to her sides.

Joe was staring at her hard as if he thought he might know her. His brows were slightly furrowed and his eyes had taken on a dark look. It made her stomach do flip flops and her knees feel weak.

Was he scrutinizing her looks the same way she was scrutinizing his?

She had been told many times in her life that she was a very attractive woman. Her long, dark brown, wavy hair and deep green eyes had gained her a few admirers over the years, not to mention her tiny, petite frame. But she had never found anyone who sparked her interest enough to get married, so at 27, she was still contentedly single.

Finally, Joe broke the awkward silence. "Well, I'm quite the handyman if you need anything repaired or if you decide to do any remodeling on it. I know it could use a bit of updating," he told her, still staring at her with those smoldering eyes.

"Well, y..y..yes," she said. "It will need a bit of updating."

"Well, if you need any help, just let me know. I live just over that river there," he said, pointing over his shoulder. "My property butts up against yours in the back."

Carly pulled her eyes off of him long enough to glance over his shoulder in the direction he had indicated.

"How did you get across the river?"

"There's a rope bridge that crosses it. My granddad had it put in years ago when my father was little. It's still in good shape and I use it whenever I come over here."

Carly nodded and looked over his shoulder again to see if she could see it from where she was standing. She couldn't.

"Well, Miss Montgomery," Joe said. "I will leave you now so you can get back to introducing yourself to your ancestors." He waved his arm to encompass the cemetery.

Carly laughed. "It was really nice meeting you, Joe. And please, call me Carly."

"Carly, it is then." He made a slight bowing gesture and turned and walked back toward the river.

"Wait," Carly called after him. "If I need your help, how will I get ahold of you?"

Joe never looked back at her as he called over his shoulder. "Just follow the path to the river, cross the bridge, then walk through the field to the house and knock on my door."

Carly watched him walk off until he disappeared out of sight.

She had a feeling she was going to like living here just fine. Just fine, indeed. She smiled to herself as she headed back toward the house.

Chapter 3

Carly spent the rest of the day sorting through her aunt's closets and drawers in the master bedroom. It seemed her aunt had not gotten rid of a single thing in all the years she lived there. Carly found clothing so old she couldn't tell what generation it even came from. She began making piles. She had a pile for garbage, one for charity and one for keeps. Unfortunately, the largest pile was for the garbage.

After stuffing the garbage pile into bags, and placing the charity items into boxes, she carried the items downstairs and set them by the front door. She would take them out tomorrow when she made a run into town to set up her checking account at the bank and do a quick grocery run.

As she turned to head back up stairs, she passed an ornate, gold gilded mirror that hung on the wall at the foot of the stairs. Out of the corner of her eye, she thought she saw the reflection of a woman behind her own. She did a double take, but only her face was reflecting back at her. She stared at the mirror for a moment, then trotted back up the stairs.

Once she finished putting away the items she had decided to keep, she glanced at the clock...11:00 pm. It had been a long day and weariness was beginning to take over.

She turned on the taps in the claw foot tub and poured some bubble bath she had found in the linen closet into the running water.

While the tub filled up, she quickly disrobed and grabbed a towel from the closet and tossed it across the towel rack at the end of the tub.

Once the tub was full, she turned off the taps and slid into the hot, bubbly water. Laying her head back on the edge of the tub, she closed her eyes and let out a deep sigh.

She didn't know how long she had lain there when she thought she heard someone faintly call her name. She opened her eyes and looked around the room. She was alone. She listened intently for a few seconds, but didn't hear any noise other than her own breathing.

"Get a grip, Carly," she said to herself. "It's a strange house and you've had a long day. Your mind is just playing tricks on you."

She closed her eyes and laid her head back again, but she wasn't able to totally relax. She kept straining to see if she heard her name being called again, but no more noises were heard.

After several long minutes, realizing she wasn't going to be able to relax, she eased herself up out of the now lukewarm water and grabbed her towel.

Stepping up to the mirror, which was now fogged up due to the steam from the bath water, she swiped her hand across the glass.

As she cleared a streaked path across it, she thought she saw a face over her right shoulder.

Quickly spinning around, she faced an empty room. She swung back around and gazed into the mirror, but only her reflection could be seen. She wiped the glass again, but no other face appeared.

That was really weird, Carly thought. *The face looked so much like my own. Well, duh...*she chastised herself. *Of course it did. It* was *your own.*

She quickly dried off and threw on a flimsy nightgown she had found among her aunt's things. It was thin and soft, and therefore, would be perfect for sleeping in, considering how hot and humid it was in the South.

Crawling into the over-sized bed, she slid between the covers and nestled down into the cozy mattress. Her aunt sure knew how to pick a comfy bed, she thought.

It didn't take her long to fall asleep. Within minutes, her eyes fluttered shut and she drifted off into a deep slumber.

~~~

Sometime in the wee hours of the morning, something roused Carly from her sleep. Her sleep muddled mind didn't register for a moment what it was, though. She flopped over onto her side and pulled the covers up over her head.

There is was again...the noise.

Carly slowly pulled the covers down from over her head and strained to hear whatever it was.

A faint scraping noise was coming from somewhere downstairs. It was just barely audible from this distance, but she definitely heard a scraping noise.

Sitting up in bed, she pulled the blankets up to her chin and listened.

There is was again...*scrape, scrape, ssscccrrraaapppeee....*

Carly's blood froze. What was that? Did she dare get up and go investigate? No. She had seen enough horror movies to know that that never turned out well for the person. She sat there in the bed, not moving a muscle, but listening for any little noise.

Suddenly, a filmy mist began to appear at the foot of her bed. Even though the room was dark, the moon was casting just enough light from the window, that Carly could clearly see the mist forming. It began to take on the shape of a person. She could just make out the form of a dark haired woman wearing a long, white nightgown. The apparition slowly raised its arm toward her, as if beckoning to her.

A scream was beginning to build in Carly's throat when the apparition slowly faded away. Carly blinked her eyes several times, but the mist was gone.

"Hello?" she quietly called out into the darkness of her room. "Is anyone there?"

Silence was the only thing that greeted her.

She dived back under the covers, pulling them up over her head.

Curled up in a ball, she didn't come out from under them until her alarm went off at 6:00 a.m. She had set the alarm for when she had to get up early for her job at the elementary school, but she had forgotten to turn it off. She reached over and slapped the top of the small device until the buzzing stopped.

Rolling over, she pulled the covers slowly off of her head and sat up, looking around the room.

With the early morning sunlight filtering in through the window, Carly kind of felt silly about her actions during the night.

"I was just tired," she told herself. "It's a new house and I'm not familiar with all the noises this house makes, that's all. And as for that mist...probably just the moonlight reflecting off of some dust. I did stir up a lot of dust with my sorting and cleaning yesterday."

The words Mr. Bloomfield had said to her drifted across her mind. Ghosts? No way. That's why she was imagining all these things.

Mr. Bloomfield had planted those thoughts in her mind, was all. It was just her subconscious creating these noises and images. They weren't real.

With her mind convinced that it was all in her imagination, she slid out of bed and quickly got dressed and headed downstairs for some much needed coffee.

When she reached the kitchen, she realized she had forgotten her phone on the nightstand, so she ran back up to her room to get it.

As she crossed the room to the nightstand, a floorboard under her foot creaked and moved. She stepped back on to it, and again, it creaked and slightly moved.

"Great," she said. "That's all I need is to trip over a loose floorboard."

She leaned down and tossed the corner of the area rug back out of the way and examined the floor to see which board was loose.

Using her hand to push on each one, she found the one that wasn't nailed down. She pushed on one end of the board and the other end popped up.

Slipping her fingers under the raised end, she gently pulled the board free. She looked it over for a loose nail, but no nail was driven through it.

She glanced down in the space under the floorboard and something caught her eye.

Reaching down into the hole, her fingers wrapped around a small object.

Pulling it up out of the hole, she realized it was a small, wooden box.

The box was small enough to fit on the palm of her hand. It was made out of a heavy, light colored wood, probably cherry or maple, she thought. It was plain, except for a small lopsided heart engraved on the top.

She turned it over looking for a way to open it, but it seemed to be locked, although there was no keyhole. She turned it over and over, but couldn't find a keyhole or a latch anywhere on it.

Tucking the small box under her arm, she replaced the floorboard, grabbed her phone and headed back down to the kitchen.

The box laid on the counter while she stared at it, drinking her coffee. What kind of box didn't have key or latch to open it?

She was just about ready to grab a knife from the drawer and pry it open when the door bell chimed.

She left the box sitting on the counter and went to see who was at the door.

Joe stood on the other side of the massive, carved, wooden front door. Carly swung it open to let him in.

"Good morning," Joe said, giving her a smile that melted her insides.

"Good morning to you, too," she said, closing the door behind him. "What brings you over here this morning?"

She started walking back toward the kitchen with him following close behind.

"Just checking in to see how your first night went in this big, old house."

"Funny you should ask," Carly said. "I thought I heard noises, but it was probably just the house settling or something. You know, typical house noises and such."

"Yeah, I imagine a house this size can probably make all kinds of noises at night."

"No doubt," Carly said. "Want a cup of coffee?"

"Sure," Joe said, pulling out a bar stool next to the island and taking a seat. "What's this?"

Carly turned around to see what he was asking about. "Oh, it's a box I found hidden under one of the floorboards in my bedroom. Weird, huh?"

"Yeah," Joe said, turning it over in his hand. "Looks like a puzzle box."

Carly set a cup of coffee down in front of him. "A what?"

"A puzzle box. The key is hidden somewhere in the box. You have to figure out how to find the key before you can open it."

"And just exactly how do you do that?"

Joe flipped the box upside down, onto it's side, then right side up again.

"Well, that's the trick. It's supposed to be hard, otherwise, anyone could open it."

He examined the box for a couple more minutes, before he gently grabbed the top of it in one hand and the bottom of it in the other hand. By moving his hands in opposite directions, he was able to slide the bottom of the box part way off the top of the box. Then he turned the bottom of the box counterclockwise and a small key fell out of a hollow section that wasn't visible when the box was closed.

"Voila," he said, holding up the key. "Would you like to do the honors since it is *your* box?" he asked her, handing the box and key over the counter to her.

"How do you know about puzzle boxes?" she asked him.

"I used to know a man who made them. He's passed away now, but years ago, he used to make and sell them at a little shop downtown. They were popular around here back in the old days."

She grabbed the box and inserted the tiny key into the keyhole and turned it. The lid popped open and she looked inside.

Nestled in a red velvet sheath was a beautiful silver, lopsided heart necklace. It was surprisingly heavy for all the bigger it was. The shape of the heart matched the engraving on the outside of the box. "It's beautiful," Carly said. "Why would this have been hidden under the floorboards?"

Joe took the necklace from her and examined it. "It doesn't look expensive, so I doubt it was hidden due to it's value."

Carly looked the box over to see if there was anything else in it, but the box was empty.

"Turn around," Joe said. "Let's put it on you and see how it looks."

Carly lifted her hair and turned around so that her back was to him. He reached around her and laid the necklace on her chest, then pulled it back enough to fasten the clasp.

Once it was fastened, he released it and it slid into place around her neck.

She turned back to him for his appraisal. "What do you think?" she asked him.

"It's a nice piece," he said.

Carly looked down at it. It wasn't something she would normally wear, but there was something special about this heart necklace, she could feel it. The thick, heavy woven chain that held it stood out against her black shirt and gave it a classy look.

"I really like it," she told Joe. "I think I'll wear it today."

"So, what are your plans for the day?"

"I went through Aunt Ruth's closets last night and I have several bags of clothes to dispose of and a few to donate to the local charity. Do you know where that might be?"

"Best place to take it would be St. Vincent de Paul's Charity House down on Main Street. They do good work down there."

"Um, could you give me directions?" Carly asked. "I haven't been to town yet and I have no idea where anything is."

"Better yet, how about I take you," Joe offered. "I could show you around town, then maybe we could grab lunch at Franko's."

"Franko's?"

"It's a small mom and pop place, but they have the best burgers in town. It's a favorite spot for all the locals."

Excitement raced through Carly's veins at the thought of spending the day with Joe. She didn't know what it was about him, but she felt an instant connection with him and definitely an instant attraction.

"Sure. That would be great," she said. "Let me grab my purse and lock things up and we can go."

After a quick check in the bathroom mirror to make sure she was presentable, Carly grabbed her purse and headed for the front door.

Joe was leaning against the door jamb that led into the sitting room. He was staring at the fireplace with an odd expression on his face.

"Is everything ok?" Carly asked him.

He jumped when she spoke, but quickly recovered and turned to look at her. "Yeah, great. I was just admiring that fireplace," he said. "Is it original to the house?"

"I have no idea," Carly said, looking with interest at it. "I don't know anything about the house yet. I would be interested in learning more about it, though."

"You need to visit our local library then," Joe suggested. "They keep records on most of the old historical properties in the area. They may be able to help you find information on it."

"I will definitely stop by there sometime, then."

Joe helped Carly gather up the bags and boxes for charity to take with them to town.

They walked out the door and into a bright, beautiful, sunny morning. The sweet smell of flowers filled the air.

Joe had driven over this morning and his old, red, pickup truck sat in the drive next to Carly's car.

As they stepped down off the veranda, Carly saw Vernon pulling weeds in a flowerbed next to the driveway.

"Hold on a moment," she told Joe. "I want to say good morning to him."

She walked over and planted a big smile on her face. "Good morning, Vernon. How are you this morning?"

Vernon lifted his head and looked at her. "It's Mr. Knowles to you, missy."

"Ok, how are you this morning, *Mr. Knowles*?" Carly asked, trying to maintain a nice tone in her voice. Why did this man despise her so much? What did she ever do it him?

"I'm just fine," he grumbled. He started to look away, but jerked his head back and looked at her chest. "Where did you get that?" he demanded in a harsh tone. He was pointing at the necklace.

"I found it in the house," Carly told him.

"It's not yours," he thundered. "You have no right to wear that."

"Whose is it then?" Carly asked, taken aback by his sudden outburst of anger.

"Who do you think you are? You have no right."

"Mr. Knowles, I'm sorry. I don't understand."

"Of course, you don't," he said. With that, he turned and walked away from her.

Carly watched him walk away from her the same way he did the day before. Joe walked up behind her and laid his arm on her shoulder. "What was that about?"

"I have no idea," Carly said.

She decided to brush off Vernon's outburst and just chalk it up to him being a grumpy old man. She was determined to win him over one day, but today was not going to be that day.

Chapter 4

The ride into town was a pleasant one. With the windows rolled down, the air blowing in on them was hot, but Carly didn't notice. Her whole attention was on Joe. Conversation between them seemed to flow effortlessly and she found the time slipping by quickly.

"So, did you know my aunt well?" she asked.

"No, not really," Joe said. "She was a bit of a recluse, kept mostly to herself."

"But you kept on eye on the place after she passed," Carly said. "I just assumed you were close to her."

"I knew her, but not well. She was kind and friendly when we saw her in town, but she never got involved with other people much. She always seemed sad to me. I just kept an eye on the place after she passed because of Vernon. He was here all alone and I didn't want anyone poking around causing him any trouble. He's so old and feeble. I just kind of wanted to watch out for him, you know?"

"I bet he appreciated that," Carly said. "It can't have been easy looking after the place all by himself."

"Oh, he didn't know I was watching over things," Joe chuckled. "You've met him. He would have considered it an insult."

"Well, I guess you're probably right. He does seem a bit obstinate at times."

"A bit?" Joe laughed out loud at that.

"What's up with him anyway? Why is he so mean and cranky?"

"I have no idea. He's been that way since I've known him. He's been the caretaker of Montgomery Manor since before I was born. I think he came with the place."

They both laughed and the conversation lulled for a few minutes. Carly was enjoying Joe's company. She was inwardly delighted that he opted to take her to town today instead of her going by herself. She could not deny an attraction toward him.

She stole a quick glance in his direction and smiled. His hair was ruffled from the wind blowing across it, but it just further accentuated his attractiveness. His long, straight nose and full lips enticed her. She couldn't help but wonder what those lips pressed against hers would feel like.

"So, where do you want to go first?" Joe asked, bringing her out of her reverie. "We're almost to town now. Just a mile or so more."

"Um," Carly stammered, a deep blush rising on her cheeks at her own thoughts. "I guess the bank."

The small town of Summer Haven was not what Carly had expected. It was a cozy, charming little town that she thought only existed in movies. The streets were lined with tall shade trees. The sidewalks were immaculately clean with large stone flowerpots set about ten feet apart. Small, decorative, wooden benches were set between the flowerpots. Store windows were clean and decorated according to its wares and old fashioned gas lampposts graced each corner.

"What a beautiful little town," Carly said.

"Yeah, it sure is," Joe said, pulling the old pickup into a parking space in front of the bank. "The community takes pride in our little town."

"It shows," Carly said.

Joe jumped out of the truck and walked around to her door and opened it for her. She slid out and thanked him.

A gentleman, too, she thought. His qualities were racking up.

"I'll let you attend to your banking business while I drop the stuff off at Vincent de Paul's Charity House," he told her, indicating the boxes in the back of the truck. "Meet you out front of the bank when you're done?"

"Sure," Carly said. "This shouldn't take too long. I just need to set up my account and have my aunt's funds transferred to mine."

She stepped into the small, but elegantly decorated bank foyer. She made her way up to a teller and explained what she needed.

After taking a seat in a small waiting area, she picked up a newspaper that was laying on an end table next to her and began flipping through it.

Her eyes caught an article that snagged her attention. *Local area woman still missing. Police have no leads.*

Hhmmm, Carly thought. *I guess even a small, charming town like this one still has its crimes.*

Soon, a smartly dressed woman called to her from a door across from the sitting area. Carly jumped to her feet and followed the woman into her office.

"So, what can I do for you today, Miss..?" asked the lady.

"Montgomery," Carly said. "Carly Montgomery. I'm here to set up a checking account and to transfer money from my aunt's account into mine. I have the paperwork here that you'll need."

She drew out the paperwork Mr. Bloomfield had given her and passed it across the desk to the banker.

"You must be Ruth Montgomery's niece," the bank lady said.

"Yes, ma'am," Carly said.

"Lucky you," the banker lady said with a smile. "Your aunt has had an account with our bank for years. You must be quite happy to have inherited such a fortune."

Carly stared at the lady for a moment trying to decide whether she was being catty or just friendly. Deciding, or rather hoping, that she was being friendly, Carly said, "Well, it was certainly unexpected."

"Well, I don't envy you that house," the lady said, with a wink.

"And why is that?" Carly asked, now thinking she had gotten the wrong impression of the lady.

"Well...because of the ghost."

"The ghost..."

"Everyone in town knows the place is haunted."

"Really..." Carly said, flatly.

"Well, that's the rumor anyway."

"I don't put much stock in rumors."

"Well, word around town is that your aunt was telling everyone that her house is haunted. That she was seeing ghosts and hearing disembodied voices."

"Miss...what is your name again?" Carly asked.

"Lorraine Wilmot."

"Miss Wilmot," Carly said, forcing her voice to remain calm and steady. "I would think a woman of your intelligence and position would know better than to spread ugly rumors. Do you know for a fact that my house is haunted?"

"Well...no," Lorraine said, obviously affronted.

"Then why would you go around spreading rumors about something you know nothing about?"

"Well...I..."

"Please, if you would be so kind, let's just finish our business here so I can finish my errands and get back to my haunted house. I have a lot of work to do," Carly said, in a clipped tone.

Lorraine finished her work in silence and when all the paperwork was done, she handed Carly her copies. As Carly got up out of her chair, preparing to leave, Lorraine stopped her. "Carly...Miss Montgomery. I'm sorry. I didn't mean to upset you. It's a small town and people talk. I meant no harm."

"I accept your apology," Carly said. "But I would appreciate it if my business stayed *my business*. I don't know anything about my aunt or what she believed or didn't believe, but I don't want to learn about her through rumors."

Carly stepped out of the bank with her mood a little dampened due to the conversation with Lorraine. She was hoping to be accepted into this little community, but if all anyone thought about her and her new home was based on rumors of ghosts, she might find herself a much bigger outcast than she had feared.

Joe was waiting for her beside the truck when she exited the bank.

"What's wrong?" he asked, noticing the look on her face.

"Why does everyone around here think my house is haunted?"

"What? Who said that?"

"The lady in the bank, for one," Carly said. "Mr. Bloomfield, my aunt's attorney, told me not to put any stock into the rumors, but it's hard to do that."

"You don't believe in ghosts, do you?" Joe asked, with a smirk on his face.

"No...maybe...I don't know," Carly said.

"People like to spread rumors. It's human nature. Since your aunt was so withdrawn from everyone, rumors were bound to crop up about her. Folks don't understand people like that. I wouldn't worry about it. Just small town gossip, that's all."

Carly was determined to have a good day with Joe, so she shook off the bad mood and put it behind her.

"Let's get lunch before we pick up your groceries," Joe suggested.

"Yes, let's," Carly agreed. "I'm starved." She slipped her hand through Joe's bent arm and they walked down the sidewalk the short distance to Franko's.

The restaurant had a rustic country flare to it. Wagon wheel chandeliers hung from the ceiling and wooden tables and chairs were positioned around a large stone fireplace. Carly liked the place immediately.

Taking a seat next to a large window overlooking the river, Carly opened the menu and scanned the contents.

Having decided on a Swiss Mushroom burger and sweet tea, she laid the menu down and looked at Joe.

"So, what do you do, Joe. For work, I mean?" she asked him.

"I'm a contractor," he told her, taking a sip of his tea.

"Like in construction?"

"Yep...like in construction. That's why I said to call me if you needed any work done. I'm kind of a jack of all trades."

"You don't keep regular business hours?"

"Nope. I just work when I'm called in for a job."

"How do you support yourself only working occasionally?"

"I make good money doing what I do. I don't have to work full time to earn a living. That's why I love what I do." He smiled at her, making her insides turn to jello.

"What about you, Carly? What do you do?"

"I teach elementary school. Or rather, I did. I don't know what I'll do now."

"What do you mean?"

"I'll have to check with the school here to see if they'll have a position open this fall. If not, I guess I'll just hang around the house and start doing some of the painting and fixing up I want to get done."

"If you need any help...," Joe offered.

"Thanks. I may just take you up on that," Carly said, smiling shyly at him. She didn't want him to think that she only wanted him around to do work on the house, but since he offered, it would give her a reason to ask him over.

"What did my aunt do for a living?" she asked.

"Not a darn thing from what I hear," Joe said. "Your grandparents were rich, so she never had to work. She inherited their fortune, so she just stayed in the house and did whatever it is she did."

"That's odd. I wonder why she never got out and did something with her life. What kept her here?" Carly asked.

"A lot of folks wondered that. She never married. Never had children. All she would ever say is that that house and that property held her greatest treasure," Joe said.

"Her greatest treasure? I wonder what she meant by that?" Carly asked, puzzled. "She was known to be wealthy. She had a huge home and eloquent gardens. What could possibly be more of a treasure than that?"

"That's the big question," Joe said. "Maybe she had riches much more valuable than the property or her bank account hidden somewhere in or around the property."

Carly noticed a slight change in Joe's demeanor as they talked about her aunt. It wasn't anything she could put her finger on, but it was there. Was he uncomfortable talking about her? And if so, why? Maybe she just imagined the dark shadows that fell across his eyes.

Just then the waitress brought their food out.

As they ate, Carly glanced up at Joe, but whatever she had seen in his eyes before was gone now, so she brushed it off and took a bite of her sandwich.

When the check came, Joe took it from the waitress. "I've got it," he said, handing the waitress his credit card.

"Thank you," Carly said. "You're almost too good to be true."

"I doubt that," Joe laughed. "My mom taught me to be a gentleman and I guess I took the teaching to heart."

"Well, I appreciate it," Carly said, reaching across the table and laying her hand on top of his. A spark shot through her hand at the contact and she wondered if he felt it, too.

After a quick run to the local grocery store, they headed back to the mansion.

Carly couldn't remember a time she had enjoyed herself so much. Joe was a breath of fresh air. Funny, witty, charming and devilishly handsome. She knew it was too early in the relationship, but she was starting to develop feelings for him. *Whoa, slow down there, Nellie,* she chided herself. *Don't go rushing into things. You don't know him that well yet.*

Joe pulled up next to the steps of her house and jumped out, coming around to open the door for her again. He reached into the bed of the truck and pulled out the grocery bags and carried them up to the door for her.

Setting the bags down at her feet, he took the key from her hand and unlocked the door.

"Thank you so much for a really enjoyable day," Carly said. "I needed that."

"It was my pleasure," Joe said.

He slowly reached up and ran his thumb across her cheek. He then slid his hand around the back of her neck and pulled her head toward his. He lowered his mouth until it was just over hers and after a brief pause, pressed his lips against hers, moving them seductively over her mouth. Heat rose through Carly's body. Her knees went weak. She wrapped her arms around his neck and deepened the kiss. Letting out a long moan, she pressed her body to his. He slid his hands down to her waist and wrapping them around her middle, pulled her close up against him.

Carly didn't want the kiss to end. Ever. But eventually, Joe pulled away and looked down at her.

"You didn't have to stop," she whispered, breathlessly.

"Yes, I did," Joe said, his lips against her forehead. "Gentleman, remember?"

Carly nodded and leaned against his chest. "I know, but...well...it was so nice."

Joe laughed and set her away from him. "It's going to be dark soon and I need to get home. I had a wonderful time today with you. I would love to do it again."

"Me too."

"It's a date then," he said. He gave her a peck on the forehead and turned to leave. "Don't let the ghosts get you tonight, bwhahahahaha!"

"Oh hush," Carly laughed. "Not you, too!"

Joe just laughed as he got into his truck. Carly watched him drive away until he was out of sight.

Turning to go back into the house, she saw Vernon standing next to one of the flowerbeds along the drive. She raised her hand and waved at him, but he just shook his head and walked off toward the carriage house.

Chapter 5

Carly couldn't quit smiling. That kiss had been hot, hot, hot. Joe wasn't the first man she had ever kissed, but he was certainly the first one who made her toes tingle.

She leaned against the door for a minute and reveled in the excitement that was coursing through her veins. She was sure she was falling in love, or at least, lust. She couldn't deny she found him incredibly attractive, but if she was honest with herself, she also had to admit he was fun to be around. She had never met anyone who piqued her interest as much as he did. She had a feeling there was a lot more to learn about Mr. Joe Fortner and she was just the woman to find out.

Finally, she headed for the kitchen to make herself a cup of hot tea. She knew it would be a long time before she was relaxed enough to even consider going to bed.

Looking at the clock that hung on the wall next to the stove, she saw it was only a little after 8 p.m. It was definitely way too early to consider going to bed.

She filled the teapot and placed it on the burner of the stove. As she waited for it to boil, she looked out the window which overlooked the backyard. Off to the right was the carriage house. Lights were still on over there and it made Carly wonder about Vernon.

Mr. Knowles, she reminded herself.

Why was so he crabby? It was very obvious he didn't care for her at all. But why? She had never met him till yesterday. What could he possibly have against her?

She continued looking out the window, admiring what a beautiful place Montgomery Manor was.

Up the hill behind the carriage house, she could see some of the gravestones in the cemetery. The fading evening light was casting them in an eerie, grayish glow.

As she peered out the window at them, her mind registered a slight movement by one of the graves. Leaning in toward the window, she squinted her eyes and searched for the movement again.

There is was. Just a wispy cloud moving among the stones.

Carly moved closer to the window and pressed her forehead up against the glass, trying to get a better look.

Was that just fog rolling around? No, it didn't look like fog. Fog wouldn't be concentrated into such a small area, it would be more widespread.

As she watched, the wispy shape slowly dissolved into thin air.

Carly blinked a couple of times, but it was gone.

The whistle on the teapot suddenly began to scream, jolting her out of her thoughts.

Pouring the hot water into a mug, she couldn't help but think the foggy thing she had seen in the cemetery moments ago, reminded her a lot of the steam coming up from the hot liquid now swirling around in her cup.

That's all it was," she said aloud, reassuring herself. "Steam rising from the ground. It was hot and humid today and the ground is probably a bit damp. That could cause some vapor to rise."

She turned to leave the kitchen when a small peal of thunder rumbled across the sky.

"See?" she said. "There's moisture in the air, so mystery solved."

Grabbing her mug, she made her way to the sitting room and plopped down on one of the sofas that sat in front of the fire place.

Looking around the room, she noticed some books on the shelves that surrounded the fireplace on both sides. She walked over and began searching the titles for a book she might be interested in reading.

As she scanned the books, she came across what looked like old photo albums.

Pulling one down, she opened it. Sure enough, it was photos from eras gone by. She grabbed up the four remaining albums and carried them over to the sofa.

She leaned back into the thick cushions of the couch and pulled the first album onto her lap. Turning the pages slowly, she looked at page after page of black and white photos of people she didn't know and had no clue who they were.

Pulling a photo of a man and woman standing beside a large tree out of the album, she flipped it over to read what was written on the back. *Gerald and Erma Montgomery,* it read. No date or location was written on the photo.

Carly flipped through the rest of the pages, but none of the people in the photos were familiar, although she hadn't expected them to be.

Grabbing the next album, she opened it up to discover more of the same. After going through the first four albums, she was about to give up and replace them on the shelf when she grabbed up the last album.

Opening it's pages, she found old, but colored photos. These photos contained family shots of a man and woman with two young kids. Carly examined the photos closely and realized that the young boy in the photos was her father. Tears came to her eyes. She had never seen any photos of her father as a young boy before. The young girl, looking several years older than the boy, must have been her aunt Ruth.

She slowly turned the pages, watching her father grow up through these old photographs. There were school photos, photos of family gatherings, photos with him and other young boys riding bikes and climbing trees.

She wiped a tear from the corner of her eye as she turned to the last page. There was a picture of her father at about the age of 17 or so. In the photo he was sitting on a couch with his arm around a very pretty girl. Carly pulled the photo from its plastic sheath and held it closer to her face to get a better look at it. It wasn't her mother in the photo. Who was the girl, then? An old girlfriend of her father's?

As she examined the photo, she noticed her aunt in the background looking down at the couple on the couch with a scowl on her face. Judging by her look, she did not approve of the girl. Why? Who was she?

That was the last photo in the album. Carly got up and searched the shelves for any more albums she might have missed, but didn't find any.

Putting the albums back where she found them, she turned to go back to the couch when her toe caught the edge of the area rug and she stumbled.

Grabbing the mantel above the fireplace to stop herself from falling, she looked down at the rug. The corner of it had been kicked back when she had tripped on it and now it lay folded back on itself.

Leaning down to straighten it out, she saw strange scratch marks on the floor where the rug would normally lay. She rubbed her fingers over the marks. They weren't deep. In fact, if she hadn't been leaning over close to the floor, she wouldn't have seen them at all. The wood appeared to be just mildly scuffed, but it was still an odd place for scuff marks to be.

Rubbing her fingers over them one more time, she flopped the corner of the rug back down, covering up the marks. The damage to the floor wasn't significant enough for Carly to worry about. The rug covered up the spot anyway.

Forgetting about the floor, Carly decided to look around for more photos of her dad. He obviously lived here as a child. He must have grown up here, but why hadn't he ever told her about this place? Why had he never mentioned to her that he had a sister? All she knew of her parents was that they met in college in North Carolina and got married right after graduation. She was born nine months later. Her mother had died during childbirth and her father never remarried. She and her father had lived a simple, but happy life. He died two years ago at the age of 48 from cancer. Until the call from Mr. Bloomfield telling her she had inherited this place from her aunt, she hadn't even known she'd had any other family besides her father.

Crossing the foyer into the office, she began searching through the drawers of the big mahogany desk, but all she found was staples, paper clips and some old rubber bands.

Moving to the shelves on either side of the window, she began looking for anything that might be relative to her father.

Nothing.

Other than the photo album, it was like he never existed. She found several old photos of Ruth and a few of what she assumed had been her grandparents, but no evidence at all that Dale Montgomery had ever lived here.

She picked up a picture of Ruth taken when she was probably in her late teens. She could see the resemblance between her and her father. Ruth had been a very beautiful woman in her youth. Her dark hair tumbled down her back almost reaching her waist. Her smile was bright and genuine and a sense of happiness was reflected in her eyes. Carly knew she looked a lot like her father. She could even see a bit of herself in Ruth.

Placing the picture back on the shelf, she looked around the room for anything else that might give her some insight into the family she never knew.

Finding nothing of importance, she let out a long sigh. Clicking the light off as she left the room, she headed back toward the sitting room.

She stood in the doorway for a moment and gazed around the room. Something seemed off. The house seemed so eerily quiet.

For reasons she couldn't understand, she suddenly felt like she wasn't alone.

Turning back to the foyer, she headed upstairs.

Taking the stairs two at a time, she reached the top just as a loud clap of thunder shook the house. Rain began pelting the windows and the wind could be heard ripping through the trees outside.

Carly hurried down the hallway to her room.

As she reached for the light switch, the power went out.

"Great," she said. "I don't even know where any candles are."

Knowing there wasn't anything she could do about the power, she quickly undressed in the dark and fished around on the bed for her nightgown.

As she pulled the silky material down over her head, she realized she still had the heavy, silver necklace on that she had found under the floorboard. Unclasping it, she pulled it from around her neck and laid it on the dresser.

She stumbled her way around the room opening up dresser draws and feeling around inside them looking for a flashlight or any candles that might have been left there. Finding nothing, she felt her way along the hallway and down the stairs to the kitchen.

Once in the kitchen, the occasional flash of lightning would light up the room just enough for her to see for brief moments. During these moments, she would scramble from one side of the room to the next in search of a light source.

Finally, she found a box of pillar candles in the pantry, along with a book of matches.

Grabbing up as many as her arms could hold, she brought them into the kitchen and set them on the island. One by one, she lit them until the kitchen was aglow with the soft, yellow glimmer of candlelight.

"That's better," she said to herself. "Well, so much for searching the house for anything about my dad tonight."

She stood by the sink and gazed out the window overlooking the backyard again. Rain poured down in sheets and the blackened sky looked ominous as another flash of lightning streaked through the dark clouds.

Carly could see the lights were out at Vernon's place, too. She wondered if he had any candles to use. She didn't see any lights flickering through his windows, so she assumed he didn't.

Grabbing a few more candles from the pantry, she pulled a plastic bag from a drawer under the sink and wrapped them up in it.

She didn't see the need to get dressed just to take the candles over to Vernon, so she ran back up to her room, slipped into her robe and went back downstairs.

Grabbing up the candles, she tucked them under her arm and headed for the front door.

Reaching into the coat closet, she pulled out an over-sized umbrella. Slipping into a pair of rain boots she found in there as well, she stepped out onto the veranda.

The wind immediately tried snatching the umbrella from her grip, but she hung on to it and putting her head down toward the wind, stepped off the veranda and followed one of the stone paths around the side of the house toward the carriage house.

Rain sliced through her robe and pounded on the top of the umbrella. Her legs and feet were soaked within a few steps. She pushed on through the storm until she stepped onto the stoop at Vernon's front door.

She knocked as hard as she could so she would be heard over the roar of the rain and thunder.

"Hello?" she called out. "Vernon, it's me. Carly."

No answer. She pounded on the door again, but got no response. Maybe he was sleeping and didn't hear her knocking.

She laid the candles by the door and took off running back for the house. She would just have to call him when she got back in and let him know she had left some candles for him.

Stepping back into the house, she again, had the eerie feeling she wasn't alone. A prickle of unease ran up her spine. She stood in the foyer for a moment and looked around, listening for any unfamiliar noises.

After a moment of standing there dripping on the floor, she grabbed a towel out of the main floor bathroom and began wiping the rain off her face and arms. She removed her robe and tossed it onto the floor with the towel.

She leaned over to remove her boots when a loud crash sounded from upstairs.

She froze as she started to pull a boot off and held her breath. Shuffling sounds could be heard, but since the sounds seemed to echo through the house, it was hard to distinguish exactly where they were coming from.

Someone was in the house, though. Who? Vernon?

"Vernon? Is that you?" she called out.

No answer.

"Vernon, are you in here?" she called out, louder this time.

No answer.

Fear gripped her heart and made her blood run cold.

Another soft shuffling sound could be heard.

Someone was definitely in the house.

What should she do? The electricity was still out, but she remembered she had left her cell phone in the kitchen, so she tiptoed down the hall hoping she didn't run into her intruder on the way.

She slunk into the room, listening for any noise that might alert her to someone's presence, but heard nothing. Feeling her way around the island with her hands, she found her phone. Picking it up, she dialed 9-1-1.

As the phone was ringing, trying to connect, she quietly made her way back out to the foyer in case she needed to make a run for it out the front door.

The 9-1-1 operator came on the line just as she passed the hallway mirror. Casting a quick glance at it, she let out a blood curdling scream and dropped the phone.

As she ran for the front door, she could hear the operator calling out to her. "Miss? Miss, are you alright? Can you hear me?"

Not stopping to pick up the phone, Carly threw open the door and bolted out into the storm.

She stepped down off the last step and dashed across the front lawn toward the driveway.

The wet grass and mud proved more than her feet could handle and they flew out from under her. She landed on her side and slid several feet before coming to a stop. Her nightgown had rolled up to her hips and one of her boots had flown off and landed several feet away. Mud covered her from head to toe as the rain beat down on her.

She rolled over onto her back and, looking up through the pouring rain, let out

another scream that was loud enough to wake
the dead.

Chapter 6

"What in the world are you doing?" came Joe's voice through the downpour of rain and a rumble of thunder.

Carly blinked the rain out of her eyes and looked up at him. "Someone's in the house," she panted, pointing frantically toward the open front door.

"What? Who?"

"I don't know," Carly said, getting to her feet. She quickly slid her now soaking wet and muddy nightgown back down over her hips and reached for her lost boot.

"Stay here," Joe said. "I'll go check it out."

He started toward the house when the sound of wailing sirens and flashing red and blue lights lit up the area.

"You called the cops?" Joe asked her.

"Yeah, while I was still in the house."

"Good thinking."

The cruiser pulled into the drive and an officer jumped out and came over to them.

"What's going on here? I got a call over the radio that a distress call came in for this address. I was in the area, so I swung by."

"Someone's in my house," Carly explained. "I heard a crash upstairs and someone walking around."

"You're soaking wet, ma'am," the officer said. "Here, come sit in the back of my cruiser while I check out the house."

Carly slid into the back seat of the car with Joe climbing in beside her. They watched as the officer entered the house and disappeared from view.

Carly shivered. She guessed it was more from fright than cold since it was summer and the rain was not a chilly one, but her teeth began to chatter nonetheless.

"You must be cold," Joe said, removing a rainproof jacket he was wearing. "Put this on."

Carly wrapped the jacket around her shoulders and snuggled down into it. It was warm and smelled like Joe's cologne.

"Ok, now tell me exactly what happened," he said.

"I went back to the carriage house to drop some candles off for Vernon and when I got back to the house, I was standing in the foyer and heard a loud crash upstairs, then some shuffling around like someone was dragging their feet when they walked."

"And then you called the cops?"

"Yes...," Carly hesitated, not sure if she should tell him the rest.

"What is it?" he asked. "You hesitated. Did something else happen?"

"Well...yes...no...I don't know for sure."

"Well, which is it. Yes or No?"

"While I was connecting to 9-1-1, I glanced in the hallway mirror and I thought I saw...."

"What? What did you see?"

"Joe, I thought I saw me...or rather someone who looks an awful lot like me, staring back at me in the mirror."

"You...thought you saw yourself in the mirror?"

"No, not me. Someone else was in the mirror looking out at me, but it wasn't *me*. She had her hands held out toward me and it looked like she was mouthing the words, *help me*."

"Carly, you had quite a scare right before that happened. Maybe it was just your overworked imagination."

"You're telling me I imagined it?"

"Well, I'm saying it's a possibility," he said. "Think about it. Do you really believe you saw a woman looking out of the mirror at you?"

"Well...I guess it does seem kind of silly, doesn't it?"

"Our minds can play tricks on us. I mean, it's a bad storm and you just had a terrible scare. It was probably just a flash of light or an illusion due to the darkness of the house and all."

"I guess you're right," Carly said. "But it seemed so real."

"I know it did, but I assure you, it wasn't."

Carly nestled deeper down into Joe's arms. She didn't believe for a moment that what she saw was a product of her imagination, but she didn't want to argue with Joe about it, so she just dropped it.

Rain was still pouring down and thunder continued to rumble when the officer came back out of the house. He made his way over to the car with his head ducked down and his collar pulled up around his ears.

"No sign of an intruder ma'am," he said, leaning down into the car.

"Thank you, officer," Carly said, squirming out of Joe's jacket. "Can I talk to you in the house for a moment, sir?"

Joe gave her a weird look, but helped her out of the car nonetheless.

Carly just couldn't believe she had imagined the image in the mirror, despite what Joe said. It was just too clear. The woman was white-deathly white-and her long dark hair was matted and tangled all over her head. Her eyes were sunken into her skull and her dried, cracked lips had tried to speak to her.

Carly and the officer ran through the rain toward the safety of the house.

Once inside, Carly walked over to the mirror and gazed into it.

"Officer..." she said.

"It's Officer Rick Burchett, ma'am," he said.

"Officer Burchett," she began. "I know you didn't find anyone in the house, but is it possible someone could have been in here and you missed them?"

"Anything's possible ma'am, but I was pretty thorough. If someone was in here, they're long gone now."

"No, sir...I mean...," She wasn't sure how to ask the question. "I mean...could there be someone in here who isn't really here?"

"I don't understand, ma'am," Officer Burchett said, looking confused.

Carly looked at him for a moment wondering whether or not to trust him with what she wanted to ask. He was around her age with sandy colored hair and green eyes. Carly thought he had a sincere quality about him and, she realized, a rather attractive face. Not in the traditional sense of him being really gorgeous, but rather a boy next door look. She liked his looks. He seemed trustworthy too, so she decided it was just best to blurt it out and let the chips fall where they may.

"Sir, I thought I saw a woman in the mirror looking back at me earlier," she said. Her words were rushed and she realized she had said them rather loudly as well.

"You...thought you saw a woman looking at you from the mirror?" He said this slowly and apprehension filled Carly. *He thinks I'm an idiot,* she thought, but she nodded anyway.

"What did this woman look like?" he asked her, squinting one eye and looking at her sideways.

"Well...she looked a lot like me," Carly said. The words no sooner passed her lips before she realized just how dumb they sounded.

"Um...you saw a woman in the mirror who looked just like you?"

"Well...yes...but it wasn't me."

"Uh-huh."

"She was holding out her hands and pleading for me to help her."

"Right..."

"Sir, I know this sounds stupid, but I saw someone looking at me from that mirror," she said, pointing at the hallway mirror.

"And when exactly was this?"

"Um...it was just when I dialed 9-1-1."

"So it was *after* you heard the noise upstairs?

"Yes."

"Ma'am, are you on any kind of drugs? Or do you tend to imbibe much alcohol?"

"Oh, for heaven's sake, no! I am not on anything and I do not drink."

"But you saw a woman who looks just like you staring at you from the mirror?"

"Oh, you know what? Forget it. Just forget it."

Carly was frustrated and she knew she looked like an idiot. She walked over to the door and opened it up. "Thanks for checking out my house. I appreciate your quick response to my call. I think I can handle it from here."

The officer was staring at her as if she had lost all her marbles. "Ok, ma'am. Well, if you need anything else, just call."

"I will."

He stepped out into the rain and ran for his car. As he pulled away, Carly watched his lights disappear down the driveway.

Joe came up the steps and gave her a questioning look. "What was that all about?"

"I just wanted to him to do a double check of the place. I was just scared he might have missed something."

Carly didn't want to lie, but she didn't feel like she could tell Joe what she had really asked the office to come in for. She was starting to think maybe she was hallucinating and that she hadn't really seen what she thought she had seen after all.

The electricity came back on at that moment and the house became ablaze with lights. Carly took in Joe's wet appearance and turned toward the kitchen.

"Come on in and I'll make us some coffee," she offered.

Joe kicked his wet shoes off at the door and stepped inside.

After turning the coffee pot on to brew, Carly excused herself and ran upstairs to change into something dry. By the time she made it back downstairs, the coffee was ready.

She sat down across the island from Joe and sipped the hot brew, letting it warm her from the inside out.

"So what were you doing out running around in this storm?" she asked him. It had just occurred to her that she hadn't seen his truck outside.

"When the power went out, I was on my way to check on you and Vernon."

"Did Vernon open the door for you? He didn't answer the door when I was over there."

"I never made it there. As I was coming down past the cemetery, I heard you scream and I came running. That's when I found you sprawled out on the ground."

"Yeah, not my finest moment," Carly said, laughing.

"I don't know," Joe teased. "You looked kind of sexy wrestling around in the mud that way."

Carly laughed despite herself. She imagined she had made quite a spectacle of herself flopping around on the ground soaking wet and screaming. "Glad I was able to entertain you."

They sat in silence for awhile, listening to the storm outside, each lost in their own thoughts.

"It's been a long night," Joe said, setting is cup down. "I better run back and check on Vernon before I head back across the river."

Carly hated to see him go. The house didn't feel so empty when he was there, but she had to admit, it was getting late and weariness was beginning to wash over her.

"Thank you for coming over to check on us," she said. "You don't know how much I appreciate it."

"Storms knock the power out around here all the time, but since you're new here and alone in this big, old house, I figured I'd better check on you to make sure you were ok and had everything you needed."

"Let me walk you to the door," she offered.

Walking out to the foyer, she pulled the door open while Joe was slipping into his shoes.

The storm wasn't letting up any. Rain lashed against the windows. Thunder continued to boom and lightning sent flashes of light arcing across the sky.

"There's no way you can walk home in this," she said, shutting the door quickly to keep water from blowing in.

"Well, I have no choice unless I develop the power to teleport myself home."

"You can stay here for the night," Carly said. Seeing the questioning look on his face, she quickly added, "In one of the guest rooms, I mean. There are six of them to choose from."

Joe looked at the window next to the door and eyed the sky. "You know what? I think

I'll take you up on that. It's raining cats and dogs out there."

"Then it's settled," Carly said. "Come on. I'll show you the guest rooms and you can pick which one you want."

They headed up the stairs and after checking out each of the rooms, Joe chose the blue and purple room. It was on the opposite end of the hallway from Carly's bedroom, but she figured that was probably for the best.

After a long kiss goodnight, Carly made her way down the hallway to her own room. Closing the door behind her, she silently slid the lock into place.

It wasn't that she didn't trust him, but she had to admit, she still didn't really know him either. It took a lot of trust to leave yourself in such a vulnerable state as sleep with someone you hardly knew. With the door locked, she knew she would be able to get the sleep she so badly needed.

After a quick bath, she put on clean pajamas and crawled into bed. She could hear the storm still raging outside and wondered if it would last all night long. She kind of hoped it would. She loved falling asleep to the sound of a storm.

She snuggled down into the covers and closed her eyes.

Just as she was drifting off the sleep, she thought she heard someone softly call her name and whisper good night to her.

Her sleep muddled mind didn't fully register it and she drifted off into a deep, dreamless sleep.

Chapter 7

Carly woke with a jolt. Her eyes flew open and she peered around the room. She was still a bit edgy from last night's events, but she didn't think that was what woke her.

She glanced at the clock. The red, glowing numbers read 9:05 a.m.

She had slept in. That wasn't normal for her, but after everything that had happened last night, she figured she'd earned a little extra shut eye.

With a deep yawn, she threw the covers back and swung her legs over the side of the bed. That's when the aroma of coffee and bacon reached her.

Quickly slipping into a pair of jeans and a pullover shirt, she checked her reflection in the mirror, fluffed her hair and sprayed on some perfume.

Grabbing her cell phone off the night table, she walked over to the dresser to get the silver necklace.

It wasn't there.

She hurriedly searched the top of the dresser, then on the floor around the dresser.

It wasn't there.

Carly knew she had left the necklace laying on top of the dresser. Where did it go? Did it fall off behind the dresser? She dropped to her knees and looked under the dresser, running her hand along the floor in case it was just out of view.

It wasn't there.

Jumping to her feet, she did a quick search of the bathroom, then thoroughly searched the bedroom again.

No necklace.

Where could it have gone? It didn't just get up and walk off on its own.

Feeling a bit frustrated at not finding it, she headed down to the kitchen where she knew Joe would be, cooking breakfast.

When she entered the room, a fresh pot of coffee was brewed and Joe stood at the stove flipping scrambled eggs around in a pan. Bacon was sizzling in a skillet on another burner.

"Good morning, Sunshine," he greeted her. "Hungry?"

"Good morning to you, too," she said, pouring them both a cup of coffee and sliding up onto a stool. "What's all this?"

"It's called breakfast. Have you never heard of it before?"

"Of course," Carly laughed, "But I wasn't expecting to wake up to you cooking it."

"Just one of my many talents."

"Seems you have a lot of those."

"Just a few," he said, piling some eggs onto a plate along with a couple slices of bacon. He slid the plate across the island to her. "What's wrong?" he said. "You don't look very happy at the moment."

"I can't find my necklace," she said, pulling the plate closer to her. She stabbed some egg with her fork and lifted it to her nose. "This smells delicious."

"Thank you," Joe said. He filled his plate with some eggs and bacon and pulled up a stool next to her. "The necklace you found?"

"Yeah. I laid it on the dresser in my room last night when I put on my nightgown, but it wasn't there this morning."

"Could it have fallen off onto the floor or behind the dresser?"

"I looked, but it wasn't there. It's like it just vanished into thin air."

"You thought you had an intruder last night. Do you suppose the necklace was stolen?" Joe asked.

"I hadn't thought of that. I figured when the cop told me no one was in the house, that it meant no one had been in here at all," Carly said.

"It would probably be a good idea to check the rest of the house to see if anything else is missing."

"How would I know?" Carly laughed. "I have no clue what all is in this house. I've never had a chance to explore it in depth."

"Want me to help you do a search? I don't know what all is here either, but we can look around and see if something seems amiss."

"Sounds great," Carly said. "I'd appreciate the help. This place is so big, it would take me all day to do it all by myself."

Carly was giddy at the thought of Joe sticking around to help her search the house. It wasn't exactly the way she hoped the day would go, but she was still happy to know he would be hanging around for the day.

"I won't be keeping you from a job or anything, will I?" she asked, suddenly feeling guilty that she might be keeping him from his own work.

"Nope, not today," he said. "I don't have another job lined up till early next week."

"Lucky me," she said, winking at him.

They finished their breakfast and cleaned up the kitchen together.

"By the way," Carly said, as she hung up the dish towel she had been drying the dishes with. "Thanks for breakfast. It's nice to know a man who knows his way around the kitchen."

"You're very welcome. It was my pleasure."

They started their search in the office at the front of the house. Carly scanned the book shelves while Joe checked all the drawers of the desk.

"Nothing seems out of place in here," Carly said, sliding a book back into its place.

My aunt wasn't much into knickknacks, was she?"

Carly found it a little odd that there weren't more odds and ends sitting around on the shelves or hanging from the walls. Most older women she knew had tons of figurines, glass ornaments, fake flowers and whatnot scattered all over their homes, but this house was sparsely decorated. Just a few odds and ends, scattered around here and there.

"I guess not," Joe said. "It'll make the search a little easier, though."

They made their way across the foyer to the sitting room. Carly noticed that Joe instantly went to the fireplace.

"You really like that old thing, don't you?" she asked him.

"I find it fascinating," he said, as he picked up a picture that sat on the mantle and turned it over in his hand. "The detail and intricacy in the ironwork around it is amazing. They just don't make them this beautiful anymore."

Carly watched him place the picture back on the mantel and move on to the bookshelves. She began walking around the room looking at the few items on the small tables that sat around the room.

"There doesn't appear to be anything missing from here either," Carly said.

Joe continued pulling books down from the shelves and examining them before replacing them.

"Are you a reader?" she asked him.

He quickly stuffed the book he was holding back into its slot and turned to her. "No, why? Do I look like a bookworm or something?"

She laughed and said, "No, you just seem to be enjoying going through the books. I thought maybe you liked to read."

"I'm not much of a book reader, but I do have a couple of subscriptions to magazines."

"Oh yeah?" Carly asked. "Which ones?"

"Just boring ones about carpentry."

"Well, if you decide to try something a bit more exciting, you're more than welcome to borrow any of the books in here."

Joe wrapped his arms around her and gave her a tight squeeze. "You're an amazing woman, Carly."

Carly leaned into his arms and hugged back. "I think you're pretty amazing yourself."

"Let's get this search finished up, then I can take you out and show you the grounds."

"That would be awesome. I haven't had a chance to see the property yet and I would love to know what all is here."

They searched the rest of the house, but didn't find anything missing. Nothing seemed to be out of place either, though Carly wouldn't have known if anything had been anyway. She decided that tomorrow she would go around the house and take pictures of everything. That way, she would have a good idea of what was here and if someone broke into her house again, she would know if something was missing.

They had even searched her bedroom from top to bottom, but the only thing that seemed to be missing was the necklace.

Carly noticed though, that Joe seemed to be searching harder than she was. Something in the back of her mind made her think he was looking for something. But that was crazy. What could he possibly be searching for? Carly realized that ever since the break-in last night, she was a little edgy. She was seeing something suspicious in everything he did. But then again, she had even suspected Vernon of being the one in the house. Maybe she was reading more into it than there actually was.

Shaking off the edginess, she joined Joe in the kitchen where they fixed a quick lunch before heading out to explore the property.

"You ready to go explore the grounds?" he asked her, as she slipped her shoes on.

"You betcha," she said.

As they stepped outside, she slipped her hand into his. He grasped her hand tightly and smiled down at her.

Yep. She was definitely reading more into things than were actually there. He was the epitome of a southern gentleman.

They followed the stone path around the side of the house toward the carriage house. As they approached it, Carly noticed the candles she had left for Vernon weren't out on his stoop anymore.

"Let's stop and say hi to Vernon for a moment," Carly suggested.

Joe knocked on Vernon's door and took a step back. Still holding Carly's hand, he smiled down at her. "You know he's not going to be happy to see us."

"I know, but I'm going to win him over somehow," Carly said.

Joe was raising his hand to knock again when the door opened. Vernon stood in the doorway with a scowl on his face. "What do you want?" he asked with a growl.

"Good afternoon, Vernon...I mean, Mr. Knowles," Carly said.

"I asked you what you wanted," he replied nastily.

"I just wanted to know if you got the candles I left on the stoop for you last night?" Carly asked. "I saw that your power was out too and thought you might need them."

"Do I look like I need your help with anything?" Vernon said, starting to shut the door.

"Hey, now," Joe said, placing his hand on the door to keep Vernon from slamming it in their faces. "Carly is just trying to be nice. Can't you say a simple *thank you*?"

Vernon looked at Joe like he wanted to throw something at him, but he simply gave a slight nod of his head and mumbled, "Thanks."

"Mr. Knowles," Carly said. "I just want to be friends."

"I don't need no friends," said Vernon, the venom back in his voice. "Now leave me alone."

With that, he slammed the door shut. Carly could hear the lock slide into place.

"That went well," Joe said, sarcastically.

"No worries," Carly said, always the optimist. "I'll eventually wear him down."

Joe just shook his head and laughed.

They walked up the hill to the cemetery.

Carly was drawn to the large gravestone that bore her great great great grandfather's remains. She wasn't sure how many *greats* of a grandfather he was and she really didn't care. She just knew he was somewhere back in her bloodline and that was all that really mattered.

As she approached the grave, she couldn't help but marvel at how large the stone was. It looked to be made of granite and was well over six feet tall. The base was flat and square and the spire reached to a point at the top.

"That is quite an impressive grave marker," she told Joe.

He looked at it, but showed little interest. "It wasn't unusual for the head of the family in those days to have a marker as grand as this, especially if they were someone of great importance."

"Was he of great importance?" Carly asked, indicating the grave.

"With that headstone, I'm guessing so," Joe said, sounding bored. "He was, after all, a wealthy man, so I guess this marker is befitting him."

Carly could tell Joe wasn't interested in the cemetery, so she gently tugged on his arm and they continued to walk.

They turned left at the end of the cemetery and walked along a path that twisted and twined through a small wooded area. On the other side of the woods, the property gently sloped back toward the house on the other side of the walled in rose garden.

They then proceeded to follow the driveway down to the main road and made a wide sweeping arch across the lawn that swung around to the back side of the carriage house. It had taken them well over an hour to walk the property.

"That concludes the tour, m'lady," Joe said, giving a grand bow to her.

"Wow," she said. "I couldn't have imagined a more beautiful place."

"Would you like to see where I live now?" Joe asked.

"Sure," Carly said, feeling butterflies flop around in her belly. "I would love to see your place."

"Now mind you," Joe said. "It's not nearly as grand as your place. My parents were humble farmers and our place pales in comparison to yours."

"I'm not worried about what it looks like or how big or small it is. I just want to see where you call home."

"Ok, then. Just didn't want you to be expecting something it wasn't."

"I come from very humble beginnings," Carly said. "You don't have anything to prove to me."

It was late afternoon, by the time they walked back up the hill, past the cemetery and down toward the river.

The river wasn't much bigger than a large stream. The blue-green water tumbled over rocks and downed limbs, gurgling and bubbling as it went. Trees lined both sides and as they came to the swinging rope bridge, Carly delighted in the childlike excitement she felt at the thought of crossing it.

"I've always wanted to walk across one of these," she told Joe.

"Then, you first," he said, laughing.

Carly stepped onto the first rung and the bridge gently swayed from side to side. She gripped the rope railings to steady herself. Taking another tentative step, she let out a little squeal and high stepped it across the bridge to the other side.

Once she had stepped off onto solid ground, she turned to watch as Joe crossed. His long lopes made the crossing seem effortless.

He reached the other side and took her hand in his.

"I think you enjoyed that more than anyone I've ever seen cross it," he said.

"I can mark it off my bucket list," she told him, laughing.

They walked through the short stand of trees into a large open field. It was obvious that at one time the field yielded corn, but from the derelict state of the soil, it must have been a long time ago.

"You don't farm anymore?" Carly asked.

"No," Joe said. "That was Dad's passion, not mine. I live here alone now, so I'm just letting the field turn back to pasture land, even though I don't raise animals either."

They made their way across the field to a small, rustic looking cabin set back against the woods. A dirt driveway exited the property to the right. Joe's pickup was parked in front of the house.

As they stepped up onto the small, wooden porch, the warm, honey color of the wood along with the small, square framed windows reminded her of a Norman Rockwell painting. Two small benches sat on either side of the door and an old woven rug welcomed visitors.

He opened the door and ushered her inside. It was small, but clean and tidy. He had just the basics, but it worked well in the little cabin. A simple couch sat in front of the fireplace with an arm chair on each side. The kitchen was off the living room, with a small pantry at one end. A small dining table and two chairs sat along the wall under a window next to the door. A hallway led to two bedrooms and a small bath.

"I love it," Carly told him.

"It's not much, but it's home," Joe said.

Carly walked around the small living room. It was definitely a man's cabin with the deer head hanging over the mantle and the dark, plaid curtains on the windows, but it had a warm, cozy feel to it that she instantly liked.

Walking over to the mantle above the fireplace, she noticed a picture sitting off to one side.

Just as she reached for it, Joe came up beside her and quickly snatched it out of her reach. "You don't need to see that," he told her.

"Why not?" Carly asked, stunned.

"I'm sure you don't want to see an old picture of me and my old girlfriend."

"No, I suppose not," Carly said. She thought it was a little strange that he had whipped the photo out of her sight like that, but she knew she really didn't want to see him with another woman. Maybe she should be thankful that he hadn't let her see it. She didn't want that image burned into her brain.

Just as Joe flipped the photo over and laid it face down on the mantel, Carly got a quick glimpse of it. The girl in the picture had long, dark hair. *Hhmmm*, she thought. *He must have a thing for brunettes.*

They were at his cabin for a couple of hours while he showed her around and then made them a dinner of beef stew and cornbread.

By the time they finished up, it was just starting to get dark outside.

"I'd better walk you home," Joe said. "It's going to be dark soon and we don't need to be trying to make our way back to your place in the dark."

"I had a wonderful time, Joe," Carly said, stepping over to the door and slipping her shoes back on.

"Me too."

They stepped out onto the porch to a cool evening. Fireflies were just beginning their dance of lights across the yard.

As they made their way toward the bridge, the setting sun was casting long shadows across the fields and an eerie fog was beginning to form over the river. The previous nights rain, along with the heat of the day was causing the fog to gather, lift and float above the river.

A shiver ran up Carly's spine at the sight. It was beautiful, but also rather creepy. She was glad Joe was walking her home. If she had been walking back on her own, she would have broken out into an all out run.

She stepped onto the rope bridge and looked down at the water. The gray, swirling fog mixed with the blue-green of the water had a sinister feel to it. It almost seemed to creep up the sides of the bridge and wrap itself around her neck, making it hard to breathe.

Sucking in a lungful of air, she quickly made her way across. Stepping onto the ground on the other side, she breathed a sigh of relief.

Something about the air tonight felt off, though. It seemed to weigh heavy on her as if it was seeping into her bones. Looking around, an unnatural chill washed over her.

Joe came across the bridge and placed his hand on her arm. "You ok?"

"Yeah," she said, a shudder running through her. "It's just a bit creepy out here tonight, don't you think?"

"No, not really," he said. "It's just fog."

He took her hand in his and they walked toward the cemetery.

Carly was too uneasy to talk. Her eyes kept darting from side to side thinking the shadows were closing in on her. She didn't relish the idea of stomping through the cemetery at night, but it was the only way back to her place.

Squeezing Joe's hand extra tight, she pressed herself up against his side.

"It's ok," he reassured her. "We're almost back to the house."

"I know, but it's just so creepy walking through here at night."

The fog was beginning to blanket the cemetery and a sudden stillness came over the place. Carly realized she didn't hear any crickets, birds, or anything that normally should have been heard at this time of night.

The tall grave marker loomed out of the darkness. The moon, with its eerie halo of light, cast a luminous glow over the stone, giving the impression it was lit up from the inside.

A shiver ran through Carly's blood at the sight. She quickly averted her eyes to the ground when she stumbled over something and fell.

Landing on her rump, she let out a small grunt as she hit the ground.

"Are you ok?" Joe asked, concern in his voice. He reached out his hand to help her up.

Carly clasped his hand in hers as he began lifting her to her feet. Just as she was about to gain her footing, a movement over Joe's shoulder caused her to gasp and jerk her hand out of Joe's. She fell back down on the ground again as a terrified scream welled up in her throat.

"What? What is it?" Joe asked, swiftly turning his head from side to side.

All Carly could do was frantically point behind him.

Joe spun around, but there was nothing there.

"Carly, what's wrong? What did you see?"

"It was...I saw...," she said, unable to form the right words.

"What?" Joe demanded.

Carly managed to gather her wits enough to answer him. "It was...her. The woman I saw in the mirror. It was her again."

"What woman in the mirror? You aren't making any sense, Carly," Joe said. He lifted her to her feet again and held her by her shoulders.

"The woman I told you I saw in the hall mirror last night. The woman that looks like me!"

Joe pushed her back enough to look down into her face. "I thought we agreed that you just imagined her?"

"I didn't imagine her, Joe. She's real and I keep seeing her. She was standing over your shoulder just now."

"You saw a woman who looks like you standing over my shoulder? Come on, Carly. You know that doesn't make any sense."

"She must be a ghost. That's the only thing she could be. She's real, Joe. I've seen her several times now. My house really is haunted!"

"Let's get you to the house. We can talk there," Joe said. He kept his arm wrapped tightly around her as they made their way back to the house.

As they walked down the hill past the carriage house, Carly saw Vernon watching them from one of the windows. When he saw that Carly had noticed him, he quickly dropped the curtain back into place and switched off the light.

They sat in the kitchen for a long time, Joe trying to convince Carly that what she thought she saw, she couldn't have seen.

"I'm telling you the rumors are true," she demanded, beginning to lose her temper. "I've seen her, Joe. Several times now."

"Ok, ok," Joe said, soothingly. "I believe that you believe that you've seen her."

"But you don't believe that saw her," Carly said.

"I don't know what to believe, Carly. I don't believe in ghosts, though."

"I didn't either till I moved here."

"Ok, so let's say there is a ghost here haunting you. What does she want? Why does she keep appearing to you?"

"I have no idea," Carly said, letting out a long sigh. "I just know what I saw."

"Tell you what," Joe said. "It's been a long day. Why don't we just call it a night for now and we can talk more about it tomorrow?"

"Fine by me," Carly said. "But you aren't going to change my mind."

Joe just shook his head and got up to leave. "I'll see you tomorrow, ok?"

"Ok," Carly said, halfheartedly. She was upset that Joe didn't believe her, but would she have believed it if she hadn't seen it? Doubtful.

After Joe left, Carly climbed the stairs to her room.

She took a quick bath and slid into bed. She wasn't the least bit tired, so she grabbed a book and began to read, but her mind wouldn't focus on the words.

Instead, she just kept going over the image she had seen in the cemetery. The woman looked scared. She had been pointing at something, but Carly had been too scared to pay attention to what she'd been pointing at. Why couldn't Joe just believe her? Why was he so dead set on trying to make her believe she had imagined it all? Couldn't he just take her word for it? Frustration was building up in her. Who was this ghost and what did she want?

Carly needed answered, but had no idea where to get them. The house wasn't offering up any clues, so where could she go to get answers?

The library.

Joe had told her that the library kept old records on some of the old historic homes in the area. Maybe she could find some answers there. It was worth a try.

She laid her book aside and wriggled deeper down into the covers. As the warmth of the bed and the weariness in her bones took over, she slipped into a dream world full of white, misty shapes and tall gravestones. In her mind, she knew it all fit together, but how?

Chapter 8

Carly rolled over and groaned. She hadn't sleep well and now she felt groggy and irritable.

Throwing the covers back, she rolled out of bed and made her way to the bathroom. It was still early morning, but she knew she wasn't going to get any more sleep.

Weird dreams of floating mists and disembodied voices calling out for her help had caused her to toss and turn all night.

She slipped into an old pair of shorts and a tank top. Pulling her hair up into a ponytail, she made her way down to the kitchen.

With a hot cup of coffee in her hand, she walked over to the kitchen window and looked up the hill toward the cemetery. The sun was just beginning to show itself on the horizon. Splashes of pink, peach and yellow were coloring the sky over the cemetery.

Carly went over the events of last night in her head for the hundredth time. The fog. The eerie quiet. The ghostly woman with a face so much like her own. Was it real or just her overactive imagination. She had to admit that all the tales of this place being haunted might have given her preconceived notions about the place. Somehow, she didn't think she had imagined it, though. It felt too real.

It was too early to go to the library, so Carly decided to look around the house some more. She really wanted to get a sense of the woman who had left her all this and try to get to know her through all her belongings that were still in the house. Who was Ruth? Was she a good woman? What happened that her father left this place and never came back? Why would Aunt Ruth leave everything to her? Why not leave it to Vernon or a friend? Ruth didn't know her any more than she knew Ruth, so it boggled Carly's mind as to why she, of all people, should inherit this beautiful mansion and the fortune that went with it.

Glancing at the cemetery one last time before turning away, a thought crossed her mind. She had wandered around the gravestones, but she didn't remember ever seeing a *Ruth Montgomery* engraved on any of the stones. How could she have missed it? Why did it only occur to her now? Carly knew why. She was still so overwhelmed with learning she had inherited this place, meeting Joe, finding out an intruder had been in her house and then, to top it off, discovering the place really was haunted. It was a lot to take in and anyone could overlook something like a grave.

"I'll go look for it this afternoon," she told herself.

She walked around the bottom floor of the home, but didn't see anything that she or

Joe hadn't already looked at when they searched the house yesterday. What was she expecting to find anyway? A big sign telling her all she wanted to know? Not likely.

Making her way to the second floor, she turned left down the hallway and walked down to the end to a large picture window that overlooked the rose garden.

Standing there, she felt a slight rush of air brush across her skin from behind her. It wasn't really cold as much as just a draft.

Turning around, she was alone in the hallway. She felt the draft again and looked up to where it seemed to be coming from.

Above her, was the outline of a door. A thin pull string with a tiny knob hung down from it.

An attic.

Gently pulling on the string, the door slowly swung down. A pair of wooden steps were folded up on the door. She grabbed the lowest rung and carefully unfolded the steps, which reached to the floor.

A musty smell drifted down out of the open space. A faint hint of mothballs accompanied the odor.

Carly climbed the steps one rung at a time. As she poked her head up into the attic, she glanced around for a pull switch for a light bulb. She waved her arm around over her head hoping to feel one in the gloomy darkness above her. Finally, her fingers connected with one and wrapping her hand around it, gave it a gentle tug.

Light flooded the space and Carly realized it was a lot bigger than she had imagined. The attic covered the whole top story of the house.

She finished her climb into the cavernous room. Stepping off the ladder, she slowly turned around to get an entire view of the space.

The switch she had pulled lit up multiple light bulbs that ran down the center of the room. Only the far corners were left in shadow.

Years of dust and grime coated everything in sight. Carly wondered when the last time was that anyone had ventured up here. Not in a long time, she surmised.

The center of the room was cleared out as a walkway with stuff piled high on either side. She walked the length of the room, passing old broken furniture pieces, an old Christmas tree, a dress form with an old dress still hanging on it, an old swivel mirror covered with a sheet and tons of boxes stacked one on top of the other.

Cobwebs drooped down from the ceiling and dust rose in the air with every step she took.

When she reached the back of the room, she noticed an old chest tucked back into the far corner all by itself. She had almost missed it. The corner was dark and the chest was cloaked in cobwebs and thick layers of dust.

Coughing some of the dust out of her lungs, she covered her nose with her hand and made her way back to the chest.

The dirt and dust was so thick, she couldn't even see what color the chest was. Wiping the corner of it with her free hand, she discovered it was a tattered tan color with gold ornamentation. The handles were leather and it had a large, flat hasp lock on the front.

Gingerly wiping off the lock, she noticed it wasn't locked. Pulling the hasp up, she lifted the lid. Dust spilled off the lid onto the floor behind the trunk. It puffed up into the air, causing Carly to burst into another fit of coughing. She grabbed one of the leather handles on the side and tried pulling the chest out into the center aisle where there was more light and more room to examine its contents, but the weight of it proved to be heavier than she thought it would be.

She grabbed the handle with both hands and heave hoed until, inch by inch, she was able to move it into the center aisle.

Sitting down Indian-style in front of the chest, she began pulling items from it. On top, she found several old articles of clothing from scarves, gloves and old hats to dresses from long ago eras. She laid these items off to the side and continued digging through the contents.

Jars of buttons, a bag of marbles and an old rag doll came out next.

Her fingers were getting coated in grime, so she wiped them on her shorts and kept digging.

Stacks of old newspaper clippings and old photographs in wooden frames were brought out next and set aside.

Finally reaching the bottom of the chest, she found an old photo album. Lifting it out, she laid it in her lap and opened it up.

The album contained nothing but pictures of her dad. School pictures of him from kindergarten through high school. Photos of him around the Christmas tree opening presents. Photos of him playing ball with other boys around his age.

She turned the page and saw a photo of him with the girl she had seen him with in the photo album in the sitting room. He had her hand in his, smiling down at her. Another photo showed them kissing, standing beside a car. Still another photo showed them laughing together over something.

Carly stared at the photos and wondered again, who the girl was. Her father had never mentioned any girlfriends he had before he met her mother.

The last two pages in the album were photos of her dad holding a small dark hair baby. These must be her, Carly, when she was little.

Pulling one of the photos out of the album, she scrutinized it closely. Yep, that was definitely her as a baby.

She had to swallow the lump in her throat. Her dad looked so young and carefree. He was looking down at the baby with the biggest, warmest smile on his face.

Carly looked at the photo again. Turning it over, she squinted at the faded writing on the back. It read, *Dale with the baby. His senior year in high school.*

Carly's hand trembled. *His senior year in high school.* That couldn't be her, then. She wasn't born till he got out of college. Whose baby was that? Mr. Bloomfield said Ruth didn't have any children. Was it another relative? A neighbor? A friend's baby?

She turned the photo back over and looked at it again. It definitely looked like her baby pictures. But it couldn't be her. She wouldn't be born for another six years.

She slipped the photo into the pocket of her shorts and closed the photo album.

Her head was spinning and she felt a bit nauseated.

She stood up and was getting ready to stuff the discarded items back into the chest when she found a small bunch of envelopes stuck in the corner of the chest. She reached in and pulled them out. They were tied together with a pink satin ribbon that was faded and brittle with age. She laid them on top of the photo album on the floor and piled the rest of the items back into the chest, closing the lid.

Picking up the envelopes and the album, she dusted off the seat of her pants and made her way back toward the ladder.

As she passed the mirror covered with the sheet, she thought she heard her name softly whispered.

She stopped and listened.

Sure enough, her name drifted softly through the gloomy, shadowy attic.

"Whose there?" she called out.

Carly...Ccaarrllyy.....

"Who are you? What do you want?" Carly demanded. Her heart began to pound and a cold fear raced up her spine.

Help me, Ccaarrllyy....

"Stop it! Just leave me alone!" Carly cried, as she ran for the ladder.

Descending the ladder as quickly as she could, she dropped the photo album and the envelopes on the floor and grabbed the bottom rung of the ladder and folded the steps up as quickly as she could. She pushed the door closed with a slam, then stood there staring at it for a long moment.

No noise came from the attic. No one calling her name.

She grabbed up the photo album and envelopes and ran downstairs.

She had just reached the bottom of the steps when the front door began to open.

Letting out a scream, Carly rushed to the door and slammed it shut.

"Hey," someone called from the other side.

Carly froze. "Hello? Whose out there?"

"It's me, Carly," the voice said. "What's going on?"

Carly swung the door open to see Joe standing there rubbing his nose. He looked a little miffed at her.

"What did you slam the door in my face for?"

"I...I didn't know it was you," Carly stammered. She felt horrible for slamming the door in his face, but then, she hadn't heard the doorbell or even a knock. How was she supposed to know it was him?

"I knocked, but when you didn't answer the door, I thought I would just stick my head in and yell for you."

"Joe, I'm so sorry," Carly said, grabbing him by the arm and pulling him into the house. "I was in the attic and didn't hear you."

"The attic?"

"Yes. I didn't even know the house had one until today. I found it when I was upstairs by the window down at the end of the hall."

"What have you got there?" Joe asked, indicating the items she held in her hand.

"Oh, I found an album full of pictures of my dad," she said.

"What are those envelopes?"

"I don't know yet," she said. "I haven't had a chance to look at them."

Joe rubbed his nose again, then looked down at her. "Are you ok? You seem a bit nervous or something."

Carly wasn't ready to tell him about hearing her name being called in the attic. She wasn't ready to share her questions about her dad's photos either, so she ignored his question and walked back toward the kitchen instead.

Taking a seat on one of the bar stools, she laid the album and envelopes aside.

Joe glanced over at them and looked at her curiously. "Aren't you going to open the envelopes?" he asked her.

"Not right now," she said. "So, what are you doing here?"

"Don't you want to know what's in them?" he asked, ignoring her question.

"I'll look at them later," she said. She didn't want to open them in front of him in case they were something about her father and the mystery baby. She wanted to wait till she was alone so she could process whatever was in them in the privacy of her own room where, if she found out something bad, she could deal with it alone until she was ready to share it with him.

She saw him glance in their direction again and wondered why he was so curious about them.

"You didn't answer my question," she said.

"What question was that?" he asked.

"What are you doing here?" she asked again. "Not that I mind you being here, of course. I'm glad you are. I was just wondering why you stopped by."

"Things didn't end so well between us last night and I just wanted to check on you and tell you I'm sorry."

"What are you sorry about?" she asked him, pulling two water bottles out of the frig and handing him one.

"I didn't believe you when you said you saw something over my shoulder and I acted like a jerk. I'm sorry. I never meant to hurt you."

Carly looked at him and saw the genuineness in his eyes. She smiled and leaning over, laid her hand on his arm.

"No worries. All's forgiven," she said. "I'm sorry, too. I must seem like a lunatic."

"You've had a lot to deal with since moving in. A new home, an intruder. It's normal to be a little frazzled with all that going on."

She noticed he left out the part about her seeing ghosts. She knew he still didn't believe her, but that was fine. Most rational people wouldn't believe she saw one. She was still having a hard time believing it herself.

"Hey, Joe," she said, changing the topic. "Do you know where my aunt is buried? I don't remember seeing her grave up in the cemetery."

"No, I have no idea," he said. "It was a private funeral and burial. I'm sure it would be easy enough to find out, though. Just take a walk up there and look around."

"That's what I was planning on doing," Carly said. "Would you like to join me?"

"I wish I could, but I have to run into town for some stuff," Joe said. "You want to come with me? We could check out the cemetery when we get back."

Carly thought it over and decided not to go. She had only been here a couple of days and just needed a few hours by herself to collect her thoughts and relax for a bit.

"I'm sorry, but I'll pass this time," she told him. "I really appreciate the offer, but I'm just going to stay here and better acquaint myself with the place."

Joe pushed out his bottom lip in a pretend pout and said, "Ok, but I'll miss you."

Carly laughed and wrapped her arms around his neck and planted a kiss on his puckered lips. "I know," she said, pursing her lips back at him. "I'll miss you, too."

He wrapped his arms around her and pulled her close to him. "Until later, then," he said, and gave her a long, slow kiss.

That kiss almost made her change her mind, but she said goodbye to him at the door and walked back into the kitchen to make herself some lunch.

As she ate her lunchmeat sandwich and handful of chips, she pulled the photo of her dad out of her pocket and laid it on the counter in front of her.

The light in the kitchen was brighter than what it had been in the attic, so she examined the photo again, hoping to be able to see it better now.

She had seen hundreds of photos of herself as a baby and the baby in the photo could easily be her. Maybe it was a relative. Maybe Ruth did have a child after all. Maybe the baby died when it was still an infant. If it looked like the Montgomery side of the family, then that would explain the similarities between herself and the baby, since she held many characteristics of that side of the family herself. Judging by the outfit the baby was wearing, Carly assumed it had been a girl, but looking more closely, it was hard to tell for sure. The child was wearing a long gown of sorts, but it could have just been a nightgown. Boy babies sometimes wore nightgowns, too. It was easier for the mother to change a baby's diaper when the child wore a gown rather than fitted pajamas.

She stared at the photo for awhile longer, than laid it aside. Picking up the envelopes, she pulled one out from under the ribbon and read the words scrawled across the front. *To My Dearest Love.*

Intrigued, Carly opened the envelope and pulled out a crinkled piece of paper yellowed with age.

Unfolding it, she saw neat, cursive handwriting that read, *My dearest Ruth, how I wish we could be together. Please reconsider your decision. I know you love me as much as I love you. Why won't you let us be happy together. I will wait an eternity for you if I have to. Love, Me.*

So it was true! Aunt Ruth did have a secret beau. Who was he? Why didn't they ever marry? Was the baby hers, after all?

Carly's head was swimming with so many questions. She couldn't think. She needed to clear her head.

Slipping the letter back into it's envelope, she carried the photo album and the letters up to her room. Tucking them under her pillow, she pulled on a pair of jeans and sneakers and headed outside to go look for her aunt's grave.

Chapter 9

Carly decided to grab some cookies from the pantry to drop off to Vernon on her way to the cemetery. She had picked up some chocolate chip ones from the store when she and Joe had gone to town.

She was still determined to win him over, but she was also hoping he might be able to answer some of her questions. *Maybe the cookies would help butter him up,* she thought.

Stuffing several cookies into a ziploc baggie, she headed out the door.

She rounded the corner of the house and heard the distance hum of the lawnmower off in the distance. Looking around, she saw Vernon at the far side of the yard mowing around the multiple flower beds and stone walkways.

Knowing her visit with him would have to wait, she returned the cookies to the house, leaving them on the kitchen counter, and headed for the cemetery instead.

She climbed the hill and when she reached the top she couldn't help but scan the area around the graves. She was alone. She didn't see any floating mists or hear any eerie voices coming to her from out of nowhere.

Starting with the first row of graves, she slowly walked past each one looking at the names engraved on the stones. There were several Montgomerys, all people she had never heard of before. She came to the tall gravestone of Rutherford Montgomery, which was in the center of the first row. Moving past it, she read several more names of people long gone that she never knew.

A sadness came over her at the thought of all these people who were her relatives, ancestors and family members that she would never get the chance to know.

Which ones were her grandparents? Great grandparents? She scanned each grave marker, feeling a sense of emptiness and loss.

She made her way up and down each of the rows, four in all, but couldn't find her Aunt Ruth's grave anywhere.

Retracing her steps, she searched each row again just to be sure she hadn't missed it.

She hadn't. It simply wasn't here. Where was she buried then, if not in the family plot?

Carly worked her way back to the first row and stopped at Rutherford Montgomery's headstone again. She seemed drawn to his gravestone, but couldn't imagine why. Her eyes grazed over the tall marker taking in every detail. It was made from granite. The engraved words were etched so deeply, they wouldn't erode off for many years to come. The stone was a medium gray in color with white flecks throughout. It really was a beautiful stone marker.

Starting at the tip of the spire, her eyes followed it down to the base, marveling at how tall it was. Suddenly, something on the base at the back corner caught her eye. Walking around to get a better look, she noticed odd scuff marks scratched across the square part of the base under the spire. They reminded Carly of the scrape marks in front of the fireplace in the sitting room. The lines were thin, shallow and just visible enough to notice them. Carly ran her fingers over them, just as she had the ones in the sitting room. Odd, she thought. What would have scratched the base of the headstone? What was sharp enough to scratch granite in such a way? She searched around the rest of the base, but didn't find anymore scuff marks.

Shrugging it off, she walked down to the river. A light breeze was blowing through the trees and it carried the scent of earth and wildflowers through the air. Taking a deep breath, she let it out slowly and took in the peaceful, quiet surroundings.

Walking over to the bridge, she carefully stepped out onto the wooden planks. The bridge gently swayed from side to side as she walked out to the middle of it and stopped.

The river was flowing under her feet in gentle ripples. She leaned over the rope railing and watched as the water tumbled and spilled over rocks and fallen branches. Birds chirped in the nearby trees and frogs croaked somewhere out of sight.

With the soft breeze blowing across her skin, the sound of the water flowing underfoot and the smell of the wildflowers filling her nose, Carly was lost in the peaceful, beauty of this place. Her mind calmed and her shoulders relaxed. She took in another deep breath and slowly blew it out between pursed lips.

She lifted her face to the sky and felt the warm rays of the sun warm her skin.

She was totally lost in a quiet calm when a sound brought her to full attention.

Cccaaarrrlllyyy…

The words floated to her on the breeze.

She strained her ears, but the voice had drifted away.

An unease filled the space she was standing in, so she hastily made her way back across the bridge and onto the bank.

Glancing behind and to the sides of her, she found herself alone, as she knew she would. She was beginning to get used to the voice calling her name, but it didn't mean she liked it.

It was still only mid afternoon as she made her way back to the cemetery. Still worried she might see the woman in the misty form, especially since she just heard her call her name again, she didn't waste any time cutting through the graves and back down the hill to the house.

Vernon must have finished cutting the grass because the lawnmower was now parked in front of the garden shed. Carly's eyes darted around the yard looking for him, but he was nowhere in sight.

Assuming he was back at his house, she headed to the mansion to clean up a bit and grab the cookies she had set out for him.

She entered the house through the front door and started down the hall toward the bathroom.

Giving her face and hands a quick scrubbing, she reached for the hand towel to dry herself off. Pulling it from the towel rack, it slipped from her hands and fell to the floor. Bending down to pick it up, she stood up and faced the mirror.

With the towel still clutched in her trembling hand, she looked into the mirror to see a face staring back at her that was so similar to her own, that for a moment she thought it was her own reflection. But the face that stared back at her was not her own. The same dark hair and green eyes peered out at her, but the cheeks were higher and the mouth was fuller than hers. Carly stared back at the woman who looked so much like herself. Fear broke out in her mind, but her throat would not let out the scream that was trapped there.

Slowly, the figure raised an outstretched arm and mouthed the words, *help me*.

A wave of dizziness washed over Carly as she spiraled down into darkness.

~~~

"Carly," a voice called to her out of the thin veil of darkness. "Carly, wake up."

Blinking her eyes several times trying to get them to focus, Joe's face began to swim before her vision.

"Joe? What happened?"

"That's what I want to know," he said, helping her to sit up.

"I don't know," Carly began. "I was washing up so I could go visit Vernon when..." Suddenly the memory of the woman in the mirror came flooding back. "Oh, Joe..."

"What? What is it?" Joe asked, concern lacing his words.

"Joe, it was her again. She was looking out at me from the mirror. She was asking me for help."

"The woman in the mirror again," he said, the tone of his voice indicating doubt.

"Yes," Carly said, struggling to get up off the floor. "I told you. I've seen her. She's real."

"Ok, ok," Joe said, placing a steadying hand on her arm. "I believe you."

Carly looked questioningly at him, but the look on his face said he wasn't lying.

Joe reached up and touched the side of her forehead. "You've got a nasty bump."

Carly reached up and felt the growing lump on her head. It stung when she touched it. "I must have bumped my head on the sink when I fell."

"You need to get that looked at," Joe said.

"I'll be fine. It's just a bump."

"Carly, please don't argue with me about this. I'd feel much better if you got it checked out. There's a small emergency care clinic in town that I can take you to."

Carly wasn't thrilled to go to a medical clinic for a simple bump on her head, but Joe looked genuinely concerned, so she decided it might be best to have it looked at just to make sure she didn't have a concussion.

"I won't argue with you, Joe," Carly said, leaning against him. It was so nice to have someone genuinely care about her. Her head was beginning to pound and little specks of light kept flashing across her eyes. A major headache was on its way for sure. Reaching up and touching the lump again, it had increased in size.

Joe picked Carly up in his arms and carried her out to his truck. Placing her gently on the seat, he went around the other side and slid into the driver's side and they headed to town.

Carly was embarrassed that when she had tried to walk by herself, the room began to spin and she had almost lost her balance.

Having Joe carry her to the car made her feel weak and helpless. She didn't like feeling that way. She had been strong and independent her whole life. Letting Joe see her that way, worried her. First she was telling him she saw ghosts, now she was swooning like an old, feeble woman. What must he think of her?

She stole a quick glance at him as he drove in silence down the dirt road. Worry lines were etched along his brow and his lips were drawn into a thin line.

"Joe?" she asked, tentatively.

"Hhhmmm," he murmured, not taking his eyes off the road.

"I'm sorry," she said, quietly. "I must seem like such a mess."

Joe looked over at her and laid his hand on her leg and smiled. "No, not at all."

"Really? Cause right now, I feel like a mess."

Joe laughed and pulled her over to sit closer to him. Wrapping his arm around her shoulder, he kissed the top of her head. "Maybe I like messes."

She snuggled up against him and smiled to herself. He was so warm and he smelled really good. She buried herself deeper into his side. "Thanks, Joe," she said. "Thanks for putting up with me."

"My pleasure."

They pulled up into a parking space outside of the clinic. Joe got out and came around to her side of the truck and opened the door for her. Helping her out, he kept his arm around her waist as they stepped into the cool, air conditioned waiting room of the clinic.

After checking in and having a seat to wait for the doctor, Carly turned to Joe. "By the way, how did you find me?"

"I stopped by on my way home from the store. The front door was open and I called out for you, but I got no answer, so I started back toward the kitchen thinking that was where you were and I saw you on the floor of the bathroom as I walked by."

"It's lucky you came by, then," Carly said, grabbing his hand and holding it between both of hers. "Who knows how long I might have lain there."

"You really worried me," Joe said. "When I saw you laying there…." He broke off the sentence and didn't say any more.

Carly just squeezed his hand and laid her head on his shoulder.

The nurse came out and called her back. She turned to Joe and motioned for him to come with her. The nurse said it was ok, so Joe got up and followed them back to an exam room.

The doctor came in within moments and took a look at the knot on Carly's head. She poked and prodded around it, checked her vitals and asked a few questions about whether she was having confusion, a headache, spots in her vision and a multitude of other things. When Carly denied any symptoms other than a pounding headache, the doctor prescribed her a mild sedative and a few pain pills to help her sleep. Carly thanked the doctor, paid the fee and then they left the clinic.

Joe used the drive through at the drug store to drop off Carly's prescriptions.

"We have about an hour before your pills will be ready. Want to grab a bite to eat?" he asked her as they pulled away from the drug store.

"I don't think I feel like eating much right now," Carly said, apologetically. "But an ice cream cone sounds good."

"Alright," Joe laughed. "One ice cream cone coming up."

They pulled up to a very colorful store front that boasted all the colors of the rainbow. Smiley faces and stars in every color were plastered on the windows and the floor was done in a checkered pattern of different colors for each tile. The psychedelic effect made Carly's head throb just looking at it.

After ordering two vanilla cones dipped in chocolate, they went out to the patio and sat on colorful round seats that were wrapped around a large, yellow table shaded by a big multi-colored umbrella.

Carly was amused at the name of the place, *Screamers*. When she inquired at the counter about the name, the cheerful, young waitress informed her it was given by the owner's granddaughter because ice cream gave people brain freezes, thus making them scream.

As they ate their ice cream, Carly looked off into the distance at the sky beyond the town. It was early evening and the sky was just beginning to show signs of a beautiful sunset.

"I was planning on visiting Vernon this afternoon, but I guess it will have to wait till tomorrow now," Carly said, lost in her musings.

"All you need to do now is go home, take your pills and relax," Joe said, firmly. "No more excitement for today."

"I couldn't agree more," Carly said, reaching up to rub the throbbing bump on her head. "I'm not normally a pill taker, but right now, I'm looking forward to them."

"What are you wanting to talk to Vernon about, anyway?"

Carly decided to go ahead and tell Joe about her finds in the attic. Maybe he would be able to shed some light as to the story behind them. "I found some photos of my dad in that album I found in the attic. I was hoping that maybe Vernon could tell me who some of the people were in them. Especially a baby that he was holding in one of the photos."

"A baby?" Joe asked.

"Yeah, he was holding a baby in one of the pictures. Weirdly enough, I thought the baby was me, but it was during his senior year in high school and I wasn't born yet. So I'm curious as to who that baby was...or is."

"What about those letters? Did you read them?" Joe asked. He shifted in his seat. Carly noticed that he sat a little straighter and seemed a little edgy.

"I opened one of them," she said. "It was an old love letter to my aunt from someone who called himself, *Me*."

"That was all that was in the letter? It was just a love note?"

Again Carly thought she caught a rise in the timber of his voice at the mention of the letters.

"That was all," she said. "I didn't open the rest of them."

"Maybe you should. You might find out some information in them that could answer some of your questions."

Carly just shrugged, but didn't want to talk about the letters anymore. She wondered what Joe's interest in them might be.

"Do you have any idea who this secret love of hers might have been?"

"No idea. I don't ever remember hearing of her actually having a male friend, boyfriend, or whatever they were called in those days. Just the rumors of a secret love, but no one ever seemed to know who it was."

Carly watched him as he spoke. Whatever she thought she had noticed in his demeanor before, she wasn't noticing it now. *It must be the bump on my head,* she told herself.

They finished their ice cream and jumped back into the truck.

After a quick stop at the drug store to collect Carly's medicine, they headed back to the mansion.

Joe's reaction to the letters was still twisting it's way around in Carly's mind. Maybe she should just ask him. It was probably nothing, but she would never knew if she didn't ask.

"Joe?" she asked, taking the plunge. "Why do I get the impression something about those letters interests you?"

Joe looked at her in confusion. "What do you mean?"

"Whenever we spoke of the letters, you seemed to get...I don't know...kind of keyed up."

"Well, yeah..." he said. "Who doesn't love a good mystery? I mean, all anyone ever knew of your aunt was that she may have had a secret beau, but no one ever knew who, or if it was even true. Now you find letters proving that she did. That's kind of exciting, isn't it?"

Carly's mind relaxed and she laughed. "I guess it is."

"If you read the rest of them, you might just find out who it was."

"That's true," Carly said. She felt silly now about questioning his motives. It was, after all, kind of interesting to possibly find out who Ruth's secret love might have been.

She leaned her head on Joe's shoulder and nuzzled his neck. "Thanks for coming to my rescue today and for taking me to the doctor. I really do appreciate it."

"I'm just glad I was there when you needed me." He leaned his head over and kissed the top of her head again. "I never want to hurt you."

Carly thought about that last statement and was puzzled. What was that supposed to mean? Why did men always talk in riddles?

Her head was beginning to feel like it was in a fog. The throbbing was starting again too, which made her eyes start to water. She couldn't wait to get home and swallow those pills and crawl into bed.

Chapter 10

While Carly was taking her bath, Joe placed her pills on the nightstand next to the bed and then went down to the kitchen and heated up some warm milk for her.

Returning to the bedroom, once she was dressed and in bed, he handed her the glass of milk and sat on the edge of the mattress next to her.

"I didn't know if you wanted water or milk to take your pills with, but I figured the milk would be fine. It'll help you sleep as well," he told her.

"Milk is fine," Carly said, popping the pills into her mouth. "It seems ridiculous going to bed this early, but I didn't sleep well last night, so I'm ok with it."

"It's not really that early," Joe said. "It's almost ten o'clock."

Carly swallowed the pills and drank the rest of the milk.

Leaning back into the pillows, she let out a long, deep sigh.

"I want to go to the library tomorrow," she said. "I meant to go this morning after checking the cemetery for Aunt Ruth's grave, but then I fell, and well...you know the rest."

"Did you find her grave?"

"No, I didn't," Carly said. "It's not up there."

"Where do you suppose she's buried then?" Joe asked.

"I have no idea. That's one of the questions I have for Vernon. Surely, he knows."

"Well, don't worry about it tonight," Joe said, pulling the covers up to her chin. "For now, just get some rest. We can worry about all that later."

Carly snuggled down into the bed and looked up at Joe. "Thank you again for everything," she said.

"You're welcome. I'll stop by tomorrow to check on you."

He stood to leave.

"Joe?" she asked. "Could you lock the front door behind you? I don't want to have to get up."

"Of course, Sweetheart," he said. He walked to the door and flipped the light switch off, pulling the door closed behind him, leaving it open just a crack.

Carly nearly squealed with delight at the endearment he had called her. *Sweetheart*. He had called her *Sweetheart*. She felt a warm flush come over her. Her heart skipped a beat and she felt a little giddy inside.

With a huge smile on her lips, she turned over onto her side and wriggled deeper into the covers, waiting for the medicine to kick in.

As she lay there, she heard the faint roar of his truck engine as he pulled out of her drive and headed for home.

The sound suddenly made her feel so alone.

She listened for a moment, almost hoping he would turn around and come back, but the sound grew fainter and fainter until it disappeared into the night.

The pills, along with the warm milk, were starting to take effect and she drifted off to sleep.

~~~

Ssscccrrraaapppeee.....

Carly's eyes flew open.

What was that? What time was it? How long had she been asleep?

She was still a little groggy from the pills, but the rush of adrenaline had her heart pounding and she suddenly felt wide awake.

Rolling over, she looked for the alarm clock to check the time, but no red, glowing numbers were shining out of the darkness.

Reaching over, she felt around on the nightstand for the clock and almost knocked it off the table.

Grabbing it before it hit the floor, she turned it around in her hand, but no numbers were lit up.

The power was out. Again.

Ssccrraappee….scrape…scrape…

She froze, listening intently.

One minute. Two minutes. Nothing.

Maybe she had imagined the noise.

She sat up and slowly swung her legs off the side of the bed.

She tiptoed to the door and quietly pushed it open a few inches and stuck her head out.

Only silence greeted her.

She grabbed up her cell phone from the nightstand and opened it to see what time it was.

3:31 a.m.

From somewhere on the first floor she heard a faint shuffling sound.

Grabbing her robe from behind the bathroom door, she slipped it on and crept out into the hallway.

She quietly made her way to the top of the stairs and stopped.

Peering over the railing down into the darkened room below, she thought she saw a small flicker of light.

Holding her breath, she leaned farther over the railing looking for another glimpse of what she thought she had seen.

Sure enough, a tiny speck of light appeared at the door of the sitting room.

Jumping back from the railing, fear seized her and she began to tremble.

Someone was in the house.

She snuck back to her room and quietly closed the door.

She frantically searched the room for a weapon. Anything she could use to defend herself. Coming up with nothing, but her blow dryer, she knew she couldn't fend off an intruder with that.

Suddenly, it dawned on her that she was still holding her cell phone.

Creeping over to the door, she cracked it open just enough to glance out into the hallway. She didn't see anyone approaching and no light was seen coming up the stairs, so she closed the door and locked it as quietly as she could.

Finding her way to the bathroom in the dark, she crouched down on the floor next to the tub and punched in 9-1-1.

The operator came on the line and asked her what her emergency was. The voice coming through the phone seemed so loud that Carly clamped her hand over the receiver hoping that whoever was in the house hadn't heard it.

"Someone is in my house," she said, barely about a whisper.

"I'm sorry, ma'am," the operator said. "You'll have to speak up. I can't hear you."

"Someone...is...in...my...house," Carly said, still as low as she could. She was terrified that the intruder might hear her.

"Ma'am, I'm sorry. I still can't hear you."

"Oh, for Pete's sake! Someone is in my house!" Carly ground out through clenched teeth, louder this time.

"You say someone is in your house?"

"Yes."

"Where are you now, ma'am?"

"In my bathroom."

"Are you taking a bath?" the operator asked.

Carly shook her head, dumbfounded. "No. I'm hiding in here."

"So, you're hiding in your bathroom. What floor are you on?"

"I'm upstairs."

"So, you are upstairs hiding in your bathroom. Where is the intruder?"

"Well, by the time I finish talking to you, he should be up here with me," Carly said. "Can you just hurry up and send someone out here?"

"We need to get some more information from you first. Where is the intruder now, ma'am?"

"I have no idea. I'm hoping he's still downstairs somewhere." Carly was getting agitated. The longer she sat there, the more likely the intruder could find her.

"So, the intruder is downstairs?"

"I assume so…"

"What is your address, ma'am?"

Finally…

"It's 18 Oak Grove Road. Please hurry."

"Ma'am, we will get someone out there as soon as possible. Just sit tight."

"What other option do I have? I'm not exactly going to go join the intruder."

"Stay on the line with me until one of our guys shows up, ok ma'am?"

"Sure," Carly said.

A crash sounded from somewhere in the house."

Carly gasped, then froze, holding her breath.

"Ma'am, are you still there?" asked the operator.

"Sshhh," Carly said. "I heard a crash."

"So, you heard a crash. Where did it come from?"

"Downstairs."

"Where downstairs?"

Carly pulled the phone away from her ear and looked at it incredulously.

Putting it back up to her ear, she said, "And just how would I know that? I'm sitting in my bathroom upstairs behind two closed doors. Do you want me to go look and see?"

"Ma'am, I understand your frustration. I'm just trying to help."

"You can help by getting someone over here," Carly said, punching the screen to turn the phone off.

"Gggrrr," she said, stuffing the phone into the pocket of her robe.

Scrunching her lips up, she whispered sarcastically, "Where downstairs did the noise come from, ma'am? Idiot."

She got to her feet and walked back to her bedroom door. Sliding the lock open slowly, she cracked the door open again and stuck her head out.

It was quiet. No noise.

She quietly made her way down toward the stairs again. If she could just get down the stairs and out the front door, she could run around the house to Vernon's and wait for the cops there. At least that way she wouldn't be alone.

She stood at the top of the steps for a moment and listened.

Still no noise.

She squinted in the darkness looking for any more flashes of light, but all she could see were faint shadows stretching along the walls.

Gripping the handrail, she hesitantly stepped down onto the first step and paused.

Nothing happened.

She took another step.

Then another.

Still nothing.

She started to take another step when a scuffling noise came from down at the end of the hall where the attic was.

She bolted down the stairs, almost tripping as her heel slipped off the edge of one of the steps. She reached the bottom and stepped down onto the tiled floor and her feet slipped on the smooth surface and she fell, letting out a strangled cry.

Scrambling to her feet, she raced to the front door.

Fumbling with the locks, she threw the door open and sprinted across the veranda, colliding with something hard and large.

"Umph," she said, as the wind was almost knocked out of her.

Looking up to see what she had run into, she gasped.

Gripping her shoulders and looking down at her like she had lost her mind was Officer Burchett.

"Oh no," Carly said. "Not you again."

Officer Burchett dropped his hands from her arms and looked her over.

"Miss Montgomery, what's going on here?"

"Someone is in my house, sir," Carly said. She looked up at him and realized she was experiencing deja vu.

"Someone's in your house...again?" he asked. The slow way he said it with that southern drawl grated on Carly's nerves.

"Yes. He's upstairs in the hallway to the left," Carly said.

"Wait here, ma'am, and I'll go check it out."

Carly wrapped her robe more tightly around her, holding it closed with her folded arms and waited for him to come back down.

After several minutes, he joined her on the porch again.

"I didn't find anyone, ma'am. Are you sure someone was in there?"

"Yes! I heard a scraping noise and then a crash, then a shuffling noise at the end the hall."

"Did you see anyone?" Officer Burchett asked. He was looking at her out of the corner of his eye and his eyebrows were slightly raised.

"No, I didn't. Just a flash of light coming from the sitting room."

"The sitting room. On the first floor?" he asked her, doubtfully. "I thought you said he was upstairs."

"He was," Carly said, getting flustered. "I mean...he is...he started off downstairs, but then went upstairs."

"You saw him go upstairs?"

"No, I heard him upstairs."

"Where were you when you heard him go upstairs."

I was upstairs," Carly said.

"So...you were upstairs when you heard him go upstairs?"

"I didn't hear him *go* upstairs. I heard him while he *was* upstairs."

"Ma'am, you are making no sense," Officer Burchett said, scratching his head. "Let's sit down in the sitting room and you can explain it all to me from the beginning."

Carly let out a frustrated sigh and led the way to the sitting room.

After explaining everything that happened, Officer Burchett sat across from her looking at her with one eye squinted part way closed and the corner of his mouth pulled up.

"Well?" Carly asked.

"Well, what?" Officer Burchett asked.

"What are you going to do?"

"I searched the house. There's no one here."

"You think I made it up, don't you?"

"Well, ma'am, I'm not sure."

"I didn't make it up!" Carly almost shouted. "Someone was in here."

"You didn't see any of this through a mirror, did you?"

"Oohhh, so that's what this is about," Carly said, shaking her head. "You think I'm nuts. That I keep imagining things."

"I don't want to believe that, but it has crossed my mind."

"I'm not nuts, Officer. I know someone was in here."

"Let's walk around and see if anything is missing or out of place, then."

"Fine," Carly said.

They began their search in the sitting room, since that was where Carly had seen the light.

She walked around the room, but couldn't find anything missing.

Officer Burchett followed her upstairs to the end of the hall where the attic was.

Poking her head into each bedroom, she couldn't find anything amiss.

As she walked to the window at the far end of the hall that over looked the rose garden, she glanced up at the attic door. Something was smeared on the edge of it.

"Look," she said to Officer Burchett. "There's something on the door there." She pointed to the smudge.

Officer Burchett grabbed the pull string and lowered the door down to get a better look.

Sure enough, there was something black and powdery smeared on the door. Rubbing his finger across the smudge, he brought his fingers up to his nose and sniffed.

"It's soot," he said.

"Soot? Like from a fireplace?" Carly asked.

"Or from any source that wood is burned in. Like a fire pit, a fireplace, a chimney. Or even the inside of an oven."

Carly grabbed his hand and sniffed his fingers.

Yep. Soot.

"See? Someone was here!" she said, jubilantly. "I told you!"

"Maybe *you* accidentally smeared it here," Officer Burchett suggested. "This doesn't prove someone was in your house."

"Ugh, really?"

"I'm just saying, ma'am."

"Fine."

They walked back downstairs to the front door.

"If you have any more problems, be sure to call," Officer Burchett said, as he stepped out onto the front porch.

"Right...I sure will, Officer," Carly said, sarcastically.

"Have you ever thought about getting a dog?" he asked her.

"No. No I haven't, but thanks for the suggestion."

"Maybe a gun, then?"

Carly just stared at him for a moment. "Why don't you believe me?"

"I just haven't found any proof that someone was in your home. Either time."

"After you left the last time, I found something missing."

"You did? What?"

"A necklace."

"Was it valuable?"

"Well...no, but…," Carly said.

"Why would someone steal a necklace that wasn't worth anything?"

"I don't know...but it's gone."

"Maybe you misplaced it."

Carly just glared at him, but didn't say anything else.

"Well, good night, Miss Montgomery. If you have any more problems…," he said.

"I know, I know...give you a call," she said.

He reached into his shirt pocket and pulled out a card, handing it to her. "This is my number if you need me."

"Why are you giving me your personal number?"

"Well, to be honest with you, ma'am, you amuse me," he said, chuckling. "This is a rather boring little town as far as crime goes and you've called us out here twice to investigate an intruder that doesn't seem to exist. It's the most exciting thing that has happened around here in a long time. It must be this place. The last time I was called out here it was to investigate a missing person and that was over a year ago."

Carly's head snapped up and she looked at him wide-eyed. "A missing person? Who?"

"Don't remember the name off the top of my head. It's been too long."

"Did they ever find the person?" Carly asked, aghast.

"Nope, don't believe they did."

"Who reported it?"

"Your aunt did."

Carly's mind was a swirl of questions. Who went missing from here? Where did they go? Did something happen to them?

"Officer Burchett?" Carly asked. "Was it a man or a woman that went missing?"

"A woman."

Carly felt numb inside. Could that be her ghost? Was that why the ghost was here? Was this where she disappeared from?

"Don't let that freak you out, Miss Montgomery. People go missing all the time. It's just a sad fact. She probably just packed up her stuff and hit the road and didn't tell anyone she was leaving. That's the rumor anyway."

Carly was having a hard time processing all this information. She needed a few minutes to think.

Stepping back inside, she started to close the door.

Office Burchett called to her, "If you have any more mysterious visitors, call me. No need to call the sheriff's office. They'll just send me anyway, since I'm familiar with your case now."

Carly slowly nodded and closed the door, locking it securely behind her.

She climbed the stairs to her room, her mind tumbling over everything the officer had said.

She knew she wouldn't be getting any more sleep tonight, but she crawled back into bed anyway.

She needed to think.

She needed answers.

Chapter 11

She must have dozed off at some point because when she rolled over, the power was back on and the alarm clock read 7:05 a.m.

Crawling out of bed, she got dressed quickly in a pair of jeans, a pullover shirt and her sneakers.

Pulling her hair back in a ponytail, she opened her door and stepped out into the hall.

She stopped just outside her bedroom and peered down the hallway to the other end.

Someone had been there last night. Someone had entered her home and had been prowling around not only downstairs, but at the end of this hallway. A chill ran up her spine. What were they looking for? How were they getting in? She knew she locked up all the doors and windows, so unless they had a key, there was no other way in.

Remembering the sooty smear on the attic door, Carly marched down to the end of the hall and looked up at the door. The smear was still there, though not as dark since Officer Burchett had rubbed some of it off on his fingers.

Yanking on the pull string, she lowered the ladder and climbed up the steps. She needed to know if the intruder had been in the attic. Had Officer Burchett searched the attic when he searched the house? Somehow, she doubted it.

Turning the lights on, she stepped up into the dusty, murky room. It was immediately evident that someone had been there.

Imprints in the dust on the floor were seen going down the center aisle toward the chest she had dragged out from the corner the day before. She could have reasoned that the foot tracks were hers, but they were much too large to be her small-- size 6-- feet.

Following them, she noticed they made several stops along the way and tracked back among the broken pieces of furniture and the stacked up boxes.

Examining one of the boxes, she noticed smudged fingerprints in the dust that coated the top and the flaps had been opened and not folded closed again.

Lifting the corner of a flap on one of the boxes, she peeked inside.

Old clothes.

She moved to the next box that had been opened and peeked inside it, too.

Old records and 8 track tapes.

Following the footprints back to the center aisle, she followed them to several more boxes and stacks of old junk piled up along the way. Nothing, but old collectibles, Christmas ornaments and outdated magazines.

Reaching the chest, she threw the lid open and looked inside. The contents had been riffled through, but nothing was missing from it.

Slamming the lid closed, she made her way back to the ladder.

Turning to take one last look around, she descended the ladder and closed the door.

In the kitchen, she poured herself a cup of coffee and sat down at the island.

The thought that someone had been in her home twice now, maybe three times, was beginning to freak her out. Maybe, Office Burchett was right. Maybe she should get a dog. She didn't want to be afraid staying in the house alone.

Suddenly, a thought came to her. Maybe she should ask Joe to stay over for a few nights, in one of the guest bedrooms, of course, just in case someone breaks in again.

She picked up her phone to call him when she noticed the cookies she had laid out for Vernon.

Tucking her phone into the back pocket of her jeans, she decided she could call Joe later. Right now, she needed to talk to Vernon.

Grabbing the bag of cookies, she walked around the side of the house and followed the path back to Vernon's place.

She only had to knock once for Vernon to open the door and glare out at her.

"What do you want?" he growled.

"Hi, Mr. Knowles," Carly said. She lifted the bag of cookies for him to see. "I brought you something."

He reached for the bag and snatched it out of her hand. "I suppose they're store bought."

"They are," Carly said. "I would have made some homemade ones, but I've been rather busy lately."

Vernon started to shut the door, but Carly stopped him. "Mr. Knowles, can we talk please?"

"What for?"

"Why do you dislike me so much?"

He mumbled something under his breath, but Carly couldn't hear it.

"May I come in, please?"

"No."

"Mr. Knowles, please," Carly begged. "All I want to do is talk."

Vernon stared at her with bitterness in his eyes, but he slowly opened the door and let her step inside.

The room was pleasantly, and surprisingly, warm and welcoming, very unlike it's occupant. Thick beige carpet covered the floor and the room was painted in a soft, muted green. A large leather armchair sat in front of a cozy fireplace and a beige and brown couch sat up against one wall. Photos of outdoor scenes done in black and white, hung on the walls.

"Did you take those pictures?" Carly asked, admiring one of a mountaintop view.

"Just an old hobby of mine," Vernon said.

"You have a real talent."

"What do you want to talk about?" Vernon grumbled, cutting to the chase.

He pointed to the couch, indicating for her to sit down.

Taking a seat on the end nearest his armchair, she asked, "Where is Aunt Ruth buried? I can't find her grave up on the hill."

"That's cause she ain't there," Vernon said, easing himself down into his chair. "She was cremated."

"Cremated? Where are her ashes then?"

"Don't know."

"Mr. Knowles, I want to learn about my aunt. I never had the privilege of knowing her, but I would like to learn as much about her as I possibly can."

"Why? What do you care? You won't be here long enough to worry about it."

"What do you mean? I don't plan on going anywhere. This is my home now."

"Right," Vernon said, sneering at her. "You'll grab what you can and take off just like the other one did."

"The other one? What other one?"

Vernon fidgeted in his seat, but didn't say anything.

"Please, Mr. Knowles," Carly said. "I have so many questions and no way of getting answers. You've been here a long time. You must know a lot of what went on here all these years."

"I've worked on this property since I was fifteen years old. I've heard and seen a lot of things, but none of it was my business, so I kept my nose out of it. Just like you should do."

"Why do you hate me so much? What have I ever done to you," Carly was about to get up and leave when Vernon pierced her with a stare that made her blood run cold.

"You had no right to inherit this place. You were not a part of this family. Your dad hightailed it out of here as soon as he could and never looked back. You don't belong here. I know your type. You'll pilfer and pillage whatever is of value and you'll take off just like Trinny did. You're no different than she was. I had high hopes for that girl, but I misjudged her. I won't misjudge you. I'm keeping my eye on you."

"Whose Trinny?" Carly asked, stunned. She had never heard the name before and had no idea who he was referring to.

"You need to leave now," Vernon said, getting up out of his chair. "I don't want to talk to you anymore. You're just like her."

"Mr. Knowles, I don't know who this Trinny person is, but I can assure you, I am not leaving. Keep an eye on me all you want, but you're stuck with me."

Vernon walked over and opened the door and stood there waiting for her to leave.

The sound of a car motor could be heard at the front of the house.

"You have company," Vernon said, as Carly stepped past him onto the stoop. "Thanks for the cookies."

He shut the door before Carly could say another word.

Carly walked around the side of the house and saw a blue pickup sitting in the drive. Curious about whose it was, she rounded the corner and found Officer Burchett standing at the front door.

"Officer Burchett?" Carly asked, climbing the stairs toward him.

"Miss Montgomery," he nodded. "How are you doing today?" His eyes traveled to the bump on her head.

Self consciously, Carly reached up and touched the lump. It wasn't swollen near as much as it had been and there wasn't much pain left. "I'm much better, thank you," she said. "What are you doing here? I didn't call you."

"I brought you something I thought you could use."

He stepped off the veranda and headed to his truck. Carly followed along behind him, wondering what in the world he might have brought for her.

He reached into the back of the pickup bed and lifted out a box.

"That's not a gun, is it?" Carly asked, suddenly leery of what he was able to hand her.

Laughing, Officer Burchett handed her the box. "It's a home security system."

Carly took the box and looked up at him. "Oh," she said, a little confused. "What am I supposed to do with it?"

"It needs installed."

"Um, I have no idea how to install one."

"I kinda figured that. That's why I brought my tools along."

"*You're* going to install it?" Carly asked, doubtfully.

"Yep."

"So, besides being a police officer, you're also a handyman?"

"Well, as I told you before, police work is rather slow around here. I need something else to do with my spare time, so I do odd jobs, and installing security systems is one of them."

He reached into the bed of the truck again and pulled out a work belt and a toolbox.

"Why are you doing this for me?" Carly asked, suspiciously.

"Because you think someone is breaking into your house and you don't already have one."

"Well, that's fair. I'm surprised with as big a place as this is, that Aunt Ruth didn't already have one."

"Me too, but then again, she never seemed to have problems with intruders," he said, winking at her.

"Ha ha, very funny. Maybe she did, but she didn't know it."

"Kinda hard to miss if you have someone stealing things from you. Oh wait...that's right. Nothing was stolen from you."

She knew he was teasing her, but it rankled her anyway. "You think you're real funny, don't you?" she accused him.

"I have my moments. Now, shall we get this baby installed?"

Carly led him into the foyer and watched as he laid out his tools and began to open the box.

"Are you going to need my help?" she asked him.

"Probably not, why?"

"I was going to run to the library. Joe told me that they might have some information on the property there."

"They might."

"So, do you need me?"

"I could use your help. I might need you to hand me some tools."

"I thought you said you probably wouldn't need me?"

"I did, but you seemed like you really didn't want to leave, so I gave you a reason to stay," he told her, smiling at her.

Oohhh, he was so infuriating. She wanted to wring his neck.

"Fine. I'll hand you the tools. How long will this take?"

"Not long. Maybe an hour or two."

"An hour or two? That's not a short amount of time," Carly said, placing her hands on her hips.

"You know," he said, laying the pieces of the system out on the floor and handing her the instructions. "A thank you would be nice. I am, after all, doing you a service here."

"I didn't ask you to, though."

"Regardless. Come on...say it."

"What?"

"Thank you."

"Oh, for heaven's sake, ok," Carly said, stamping her foot. "Thank you."

"There. Was that so bad?"

Carly just glared at him.

He got busy cutting a hole in the wall next to the door to run the wiring while she stood off to the side and watched.

The muscles in his back and upper arms rippled under the shirt he was wearing as he sawed the hole in the wall.

Carly was suddenly very aware of just how attractive he really was. Being out of uniform, she could see that he was very well built, rather muscular even. Her eyes trailed down his back from his shoulders to his arms.

Then a little lower to his waistline.

Then a little lower…

Oh, good heavens, was she checking out his butt? What has gotten into her? She quickly turned her head to the side, but not before he caught her gaze.

"You alright there, Miss Montgomery?"

"Y..y..yes, I'm fine. Why?" She began fanning herself with the instructions paper he had handed her. "It's just a bit warm in here today," she said, still not able to look him in the face.

"It's actually quite comfortable in here today, ma'am. But you are rather red and sweaty looking. If you're hot, why don't you step outside onto the porch."

She shot him a glaring look. "If it's hot in here, it'll be twenty degrees hotter out there. How is that supposed to help?"

"Well, you could always stop staring at my butt if it makes you that hot."

Carly's eyes shot up to his face and she blushed a thousand shades of red.

"I didn't...no...what?...you're insane. I would never..." Carly couldn't wrap her tongue around the words. Instead, she threw the instructions paper down and stomped off to the kitchen.

As she was storming off, she could hear Officer Burchett laughing at her.

She grabbed a bottle of water out of the frig and laid it against her neck. She was still feeling a bit warm from her inappropriate ogling of the officer.

How dare he make fun of her? Wait...How dare *he*? She was the one caught ogling *him*. Oh, how embarrassing.

She had to admit, at least to herself anyway, that Officer Burchett was indeed a very attractive man. But Joe was much more so. Joe didn't infuriate her the way Officer Burchett did. He didn't tease her. He didn't make her feel ridiculous about her intruder or the ghost. Joe was who she was interested in. All she felt for Officer Burchett was a tiny bit of lust was all. Did that make her a bad person? She hoped not.

Carly sat in the kitchen for a long time pondering why she had ogled the officer. She was extremely attracted to Joe, so why had she even noticed Officer Burchett? The thought troubled her, but she had bigger things to worry about right now. Like going to the library and looking for some answers.

Some time later, Officer Burchett came into the kitchen. "All done," he said. "Come on out here and let me show you how it works."

Carly followed him out to the foyer, careful not to look at his butt on the way.

"It's a simple system, but it should work just fine as an alert to someone's presence if they come near the house."

He helped her set the code and showed her how to turn it off and on. He then led her outside and showed her where he had placed the cameras and motion sensors.

"Any questions?" he asked her.

"No, it seems pretty simple," she said, avoiding his eyes.

"See? It didn't take me that long to install it, either. You have plenty of time to get to the library. It's not even noon yet."

"Thanks for this, Officer Burchett," she said, meaning it. "I really do appreciate it. You might not believe me, but I did find proof that someone was in the house last night."

"Please, call me Rick. I think we're past the formalities."

"Ok, then," she said. "Rick."

"You say you have proof? What is it?"

"I checked out the attic this morning. I found foot tracks and some of the boxes were opened and gone through."

"Do you want me to take a look?" he asked, looking a bit concerned.

"No," Carly said. "If anything was taken, I wouldn't know it anyway. There's so much junk up there."

"I'm hoping with the security system, that next time your intruder comes back, you'll know before he gets into the house and you can call me."

"I hope he doesn't come back at all."

"You on your way to the library now?" he asked her.

"Yes. I'm hoping to learn something about this place and about my aunt. Vernon's been no help."

"Mind if I go with you?"

"Why do you want to come?" Carly asked, surprised.

"Truthfully? I have nothing better to do right now."

Carly couldn't help, but laugh. "I guess that's as good an excuse as any," she said.

"I'll drive," he said. "That way you can have all the time you want to ogle me on the drive down."

Carly reached out to slap his arm. He ducked out of the way and started laughing. Carly couldn't help herself. She burst out laughing too. "Hey, in my defense, those jeans are rather flattering. I wasn't looking at your butt. I was checking out those Levi's."

Rick laughed again and opened the front door, allowing her to step out ahead of him. "Rrriiiggghhhttt..." he said.

"If you mention it to anyone, I'll just deny it," Carly said, still laughing. "I can't believe you caught me."

"It was hard to miss," Rick said. "You were drooling and everything."

"Oh, hush up," Carly said, climbing into the pickup. "I was not."

"Could have fooled me," Rick said, as he crawled into the driver's seat. He gunned the engine, then pulling out of the drive.

Carly wasn't sure how she went from being angry and infuriated at Rick, to laughing with him at her own expense.

They exchanged easy banter as they drove into town.

Carly was seeing a side of Rick that she had not seen while he was in uniform. This Rick was relaxed and fun loving. His sense of humor intrigued her. He didn't seem to let much ruffle his feathers. She was beginning to realize that she genuinely liked this man. As a friend, of course.

Chapter 12

The library was small, but laid out in such a way as to appear larger than it was. Tall shelves filled with books lined the walls and the welcome desk was centered in the middle of the room. Small tables and chairs were placed every few feet around the room.

Carly stepped up to the counter while Rick roamed around looking at different books on the shelves.

A short, plumb woman with cropped, gray hair waddled up to the counter. "Howdy there," she said, as way of a greeting. "What can I do for you?" She suddenly gasped and threw her hand up to her throat. "Trinny?" she asked, staring hard at Carly.

Carly stared at the woman for a second, stunned. "N...n...no," she said. "My name's Carly. Carly Montgomery."

The woman blinked several times and relaxed. "Oh, I'm so sorry," she said. "You look so much like a young lady who used to come in here all the time."

Rick heard the exchange between the two women and came over to see what was going on.

"You knew Trinny?" Carly asked her.

"Oh yes, very sweet woman," Sue said.

"Did you know my Aunt Ruth? Do you know anything about Montgomery Manor?" Carly asked, excitement building in her.

"Yes, I knew your aunt and I've heard plenty of tales about Montgomery Manor over the years," Sue said, smiling warmly at her.

"Can I ask you some questions, then?" Carly asked, hope rising in her.

The woman, who was probably in her mid sixties, nodded. "Let's have a seat over there, though," she said, indicating one of the tables nearest the welcome desk. "My old legs just can't take standing for too long these days."

Carly looked at Rick and he nodded and followed the women to the table.

He pulled out the chair for the librarian and took a seat himself. "You know, if we're going to be sitting here for awhile, a refreshment might be nice. It is almost lunch time."

Carly stared at him, completely dumbfounded. Then, "Oh, and I suppose you want donuts and coffee?" She laughed to herself at the old cop joke.

"As a matter of fact, there's a small bakery next door. Why don't you whip on over there and grab us some before we get started?"

Carly looked at him like he had lost his mind. "You're serious?"

He turned to the woman next to him and asked, "What do you think, Sue? Want some donuts and coffee?"

"Why, that would be nice," she said, nodding her head vigorously. "Yes, please."

Carly shook her head in disbelief.

Pointing her finger in Rick's face, she said, "You better be here when I get back. Don't you dare leave while I'm gone. You're my ride home, you know."

Rick saluted her and chuckled. "I'll be right here when you get back. I don't want to miss out on free donuts and coffee."

Carly mumbled under her breath all the things she'd like to do to Rick as she walked out the door and across the street to the bakery.

After ordering a half dozen assorted donuts and three coffees, she made her way back to the library.

"I didn't know what kind you wanted, so I just got an assortment," she said, sliding the box across the table toward Rick.

She set the coffees down on the table and pulled up a seat in front of Sue.

"Before we get started, introductions are in order, I think," Rick said. "Carly, this is Sue Langston, the local librarian. Mom, this is Carly, the new owner of Montgomery Manor."

Carly shook Sue's hand while she gave Rick a glaring look. "Mom? She's your mom?" Carly started laughing. "That's why you wanted to come to the library with me? To see your mom?"

"Well, it's not every day I get to come to the library. Besides, I wanted to hear all the juicy gossip about Montgomery Manor."

Carly laughed, shaking her head. "You are something else."

"So, my dear, what do you want to know about Montgomery Manor? I'll answer whatever questions I can," Sue said.

Carly was so relieved that someone was finally going to be able to answer some of her questions that she almost starting crying.

Almost.

"How well did you know my aunt?" she asked Sue.

"As well as anyone else around here, I guess," Sue said. "She wasn't much of a social person in her later years."

"How long had you known her?"

"Oh my, since grade school at least. She came from a wealthy family and was raised to believe that she was better than us lower class families, but she was always nice enough to me."

"Can you tell me a little bit about what you knew of her?" Carly asked, leaning forward in her seat a little.

"She stuck mostly to herself. She didn't have a lot of friends, but I think that was because she thought of herself too highly and none of us were good enough for her. Once we reached high school, she became even more distant toward the rest of us. It was rumored she had a secret lover, but no one was ever able to prove it."

"Did anyone know who this secret lover might be?" Carly asked.

"No one could ever figure it out. Some say it was a young man who would pass through town about once a month. He was a traveling salesman. Vacuum cleaners, I believe. Others said it was a local boy from school, but no one ever saw her with a boy while at school or anywhere else for that matter. That's why it was always just a rumor. She never married though, so maybe there never had been anyone. Sad, really. She was a real looker when she was young. In fact, you resemble her somewhat. Especially around the eyes."

"Did she ever have any kids?" Carly asked her.

"Why, no," Sue said, confused. "She never married, remember?"

Carly told her about the picture of her dad holding the baby and how she thought it might have been Ruth's.

"Oh dear," Sue said. "You really don't know, do you?"

"Know what?" Carly asked, a feeling of unease coming over her.

"That baby wasn't Ruth's. It was your dad's child."

Carly almost fell out of her seat. Her head began to spin and she felt sick to her stomach.

"W..what? My dad's? How...who…?" Carly's head was spinning and her stomach did a somersault. Was this true?

"You better sit tight, honey. I have a lot to tell you."

Rick laid his hand on his mother's arm in a loving manner. "Mom grew up around here and knows a lot of the local gossip. People love nothing more than coming to the library to gossip and talk about everything that goes on around here. This library is the equivalent of a local bar. I love her, but she knows more about things that go on around here than anybody has a right to."

Sue clucked her tongue at him and chuckled. "It's not my fault that people like to talk to me. I don't ask for the latest gossip, they just tell it to me."

Rick put his arm around Sue's shoulders and gave her a gentle squeeze. "Love you, Mom."

"Love you, too, son," she said, pinching his cheek.

Carly knew instantly that she liked this woman. She seemed kindhearted, gentle and down to earth. "Please, Mrs. Langston, tell me everything you can," she said.

Sue adjusted herself in her seat and her expression grew serious as she began to tell Carly what she knew. "Let me start with your dad. First of all, there was a large gap in years between your aunt and your father. Your grandparents thought Ruth was destined to be an only child, but then, when Ruth was about fifteen or so, your dad came along. Took them by surprise, he did. Well now, Ruth, being the only child for so long, was spoiled and thought herself better than most. When your dad reached high school, he began dating a girl, Vera Carter. Ruth didn't like it none. In fact, not at all. You see, Vera was from the wrong side of the tracks. Her mother was a waitress at the diner and her daddy worked in the factory on the outskirts of town. Vera wasn't good enough for Dale Montgomery, as far as Ruth was concerned. She ragged him horribly about dating her. She was downright mean and nasty to poor Vera, but your daddy didn't care. He loved Vera and continued to date her until one day they found out she was pregnant. In those days, that was not something to be proud of. Ruth thought for sure it would bring shame to their family, so she did everything in her power to break them up. She didn't want your daddy to marry that girl and she didn't want anyone knowing about that baby. When the baby came, that still didn't change Ruth's mind any. No one knows exactly what she said or did to Vera, but one day, Vera just up and moved away taking the baby with her. Your grandparents gave approval to Ruth's actions. Your daddy was so upset, that he stormed out of the house one day and never came back. Your grandparents tried for years to coax him back, offering him money, a job, whatever it took, but he never came back. As far as the town knew, he was gone for good."

Carly shook her head sadly. "Whatever happened to Vera and the baby?"

Sue looked at Rick. He nodded to her, so she continued. "Vera never came back, but Trinny did. She's your half sister, you know."

Carly felt the air leave her lungs as the realization hit her. She had a sister. A half sister named Trinny. "Where is she now? Rick told me she went missing? What happened?" The words tumbled out so fast, Carly wasn't sure she'd even asked them.

"Trinny showed up at your aunt's house out of the blue, a little over a year ago. She told your aunt who she was, expecting your aunt to slam the door in her face. But instead, Ruth took her in and gave her a job as her caregiver. She told Trinny that she felt bad that she had run her mother off and if she could go back and change the past, she would. Trinny's mother had passed away in a car accident a few months before she showed up. That's why Trinny came back. She was looking for family."

Sue took a deep breath before continuing. "One day, Trinny just disappeared. Several items of worth went missing along with her. Your aunt assumed she had loaded up a bunch of costly items and taken off, but she felt she needed to report it, so she called the cops. When Trinny couldn't be found, they listed her as missing. She's never come back since. It broke your aunt's heart. She really seemed to have taken a deep liking to the girl."

Carly looked at Rick. "Did they ever do a search for her? Did anyone ever try to find her?"

"Yes, but nothing was ever found. Not a trace. It was like she vanished into thin air." Rick said.

"I think I know where she is," Carly said. "I think she's the ghost haunting the mansion."

Sue looked at her strangely. "That's weird," she said. "After Trinny disappeared, your aunt believed her house became haunted. Claimed she kept seeing a woman in the mirrors or floating around the house. Everyone just chalked it up to her being old and senile."

"I think she was actually seeing the same things I've seen," Carly said. "Ever since I moved into that house, I've been seeing a woman in the mirrors that looks so much like me. It must be Trinny."

"Whoa," Rick said. "Slow down there. Are you insinuating that Trinny is dead?"

"It's the only thing that makes sense," Carly said. "All I know is that the woman I keep seeing looks a whole lot like me and we know that Trinny is missing. Don't you see the connection?"

Rick looked at her skeptically. "Let's not jump to conclusions. Just cause no one has been able to find Trinny, doesn't mean she's dead. She could be anywhere."

Carly wasn't going to be put off. "The woman keeps calling out to me. She knows my name."

"I'm not sure Trinny knew of your existence, honey," Sue said. "Your aunt didn't know about you till after Trinny disappeared."

"What do you mean?" asked Carly.

"Trinny was going to inherit Montgomery Manor, but when she disappeared, your aunt didn't have anyone to leave it to. She never knew what became of your father, so she hired a private investigator to find him. That's how she found out about you," Sue told her.

"I don't remember a private investigator ever contacting me," Carly said.

"He wouldn't have had to," Rick said. "His job was to find your father and any possible children your father might have had. Once he found out about you, he reported back to Ruth. That's why you inherited the manor. You were her only known living relative."

Carly sat there quietly for moment. This was a lot of information to process, but she still wanted to learn more.

"So, if Trinny were still alive...or around somewhere...she would have been the one to inherit the place?"

"Yes," Sue said. "By rights, she was the oldest of Dale's children, so it would have fallen to her first."

"I think Trinny is trying to reach out to me," Carly said, softly.

"Why do you think that?" Sue asked.

"I've heard her call my name and whenever I see her, she's holding out her hand to me and mouthing the words, *help me*."

"I'm still having a hard time believing in ghosts," Rick said. "There has to be a logical explanation."

"Now Rick," said Sue. "Just because you don't believe, doesn't mean they don't exist. If Carly says she's seen one, then we have to believe that she has."

Rick just raised his eyebrows and shook his head. "Whatever," he mumbled.

"What do you suppose she wants, dear?" Sue asked Carly.

"I have no idea," Carly said. "Every time I've seen her, I've gotten scared and run."

"That's how we met, Mom," Rick said, looking over at Carly and chuckling. "The first time I was called over to her place, she was wrestling around in the mud in just her nightgown claiming to have seen someone in her mirror."

Carly gave him a hard stare. "You're an idiot."

"But, it's true, though," Rick laughed.

"Rick, stop making fun of her," Sue said. "I imagine that was rather scary, seeing someone in a mirror who didn't belong there."

"Thank you, Sue," Carly said, still glaring at Rick. "It was."

"So what are you going to do about your ghost?" Rick asked.

"I have no idea," Carly said.

"You need to go see Madam Hornbeck," Sue said.

"Mother, no," Rick said.

Both Sue and Carly ignored him.

"Whose Madam Hornbeck?" Carly asked, her interested peaked.

"Don't go there, Mom," Rick said, exasperated. "That woman's a nut job."

Ignoring Rick, Sue told Carly, "She's the local psychic. She has a place over on Locust Road, just outside the city limits. She supposedly can communicate with the dead. Maybe you need to pay her a visit. She might be able to tell you what you need to do."

Rick let out a low groan and rolled his eyes.

"Do you happen to have her number?" Carly asked.

"She doesn't use a phone, dear," Sue told her. "You'll just have to stop in over there. It's the third house down on the left. Pink house with white shudders. You can't miss it."

"On the bright side," Rick said, sarcastically. "She should know you're coming."

Carly and Sue both laughed.

After they had polished off the donuts, Carly rose from her seat. "I guess I should be getting back to the house. It was so nice to meet you, Sue."

"Same here, dear," Sue said. "Stop back in sometime and we can sit around and talk some more."

Rick held the chair out for his mother as she stood up, then gave her a quick peck on the cheek before turning to Carly and saying, "I suppose you want me to take you home? You don't feel like walking? It is a really nice day, after all."

Carly shook her fist at him playfully. "You are insufferable," she said laughing, as they headed for the door.

They pulled out of the library parking lot and headed out of town toward Carly's place.

As they passed the local hardware store, Carly saw Joe's truck parked outside.

She had been so engrossed in learning about her aunt and father, that she had totally forgotten about him.

Darting a guilty glance at Rick, she pulled out her cell phone and typed out a short message to Joe asking him to give her a call when he had the chance.

She hit *send* and stuffed the phone back in her pocket.

"So why does your mother have a different last name then you?" Carly asked Rick.

"She and my dad divorced when I was little," Rick explained. "She married Toby

Langston, the local Postmaster, a couple of years later."

"So a step-dad, huh?"

"Yeah, but he's cool. He's been really good to my mom and me, so I've always considered him my second dad."

"I'm so glad to hear that," Carly said. "You seem to have a good relationship with your mom."

"Yeah, Mom's the greatest," Rick said. "Couldn't have asked for a better one."

"You should have told me your mom was the librarian," she scolded him.

"What...and miss the look on your face? Not a chance," Rick said, chuckling.

"You are such a jerk," Carly laughed.

She realized she was having a really good time with him. Even though he tormented her and teased her a lot, she found him to be easy to be around and a genuinely nice guy.

Guilt washed over her. What about Joe? Joe was Joe. He was gorgeous and she really got along well with him, too. Just because she got distracted today learning about her family didn't mean she hadn't thought of him. She had. She was thinking about him now. She made a mental note to make sure to call him as soon as she got home, if she didn't hear from him first.

"Hey," Rick said. "I need to make a quick stop at Randal Paul's house and drop off some items of his that I borrowed last week. Do you mind? It's on the way."

Carly was anxious to get home, but nodded her head and said, "That's fine."

A couple of miles from Carly's place, Rick pulled off the road and drove down a short drive to a large, colonial mansion that stood in the middle of an open field.

Carly watched as Rick slid out of the truck and jumped the steps up onto the porch.

An elderly man opened the door and warmly greeted Rick. He gave Carly a quick wave and turned his attention back to Rick again.

Rick handed him a small box that he had grabbed out of the bed of his truck and jogged back to the pickup.

"All set," he said, starting the engine. "By the way, Randal is your nearest neighbor, except for Joe, who lives behind you, of course."

"He seemed like a nice man," Carly said, just to have something to say.

"He is."

They drove the last two miles in silence. Carly was still trying to absorb the information she had learned from Sue, and Rick seemed lost in his own thoughts, as well.

When they pulled up to the house, Carly noticed that Joe was parked in the drive, waiting for her. He must have passed by on the road while she and Rick had stopped at Randal Paul's place.

Rick pulled up next to Joe and jumped out, coming around to Carly's side of the truck to open the door for her.

Joe was leaning against the hood of his truck and didn't seem too happy to find Carly with Rick.

Rick walked over and stuck his hand out to Joe, "Afternoon, Joe," he said. "How've you been?"

Carly could have cut the tension with a knife.

Joe ignored Rick's hand, but said, "Fine, Rick. You?" He didn't wait for an answer as he walked past Rick to stand beside Carly.

"Well," Rick said, looking slightly uncomfortable. "I guess I'll head home and see what I can get into to." He nodded toward Carly. "Carly, I'll see you later, then," he said. "Joe." He nodded toward Joe, then scooted back into the driver's seat of his truck and pulled out of the drive and disappeared down the road.

"What was that all about," Joe said, his voice low and accusing.

"What? Rick? Nothing."

"Why were you out with him?"

"I wasn't *out with him*. He stopped by this morning and installed a security system. I had to run to the library and he offered to take me. End of story."

"He put in a security system?" Joe asked.

"Yes," Carly said. "Come on in and I'll show you." She grabbed him by the hand and led him into the foyer.

Joe examined the system and listened patiently while Carly explained how it worked.

"Why did he think you needed a security system?" he asked, when she had finished explaining it to him.

"Ohhhh, I forgot to tell you. I meant to call you this morning, but I stopped over at Vernon's and while I was there, Rick came and then we went to the library..." She realized she was rambling, but for some reason she was feeling a bit giddy. She knew it was because she shouldn't have been out with Rick and Joe knew it. "Anyway," she continued. "I woke up in the middle of the night and someone was in my house again. I called 9-1-1 and Rick was the one who came to answer the call...again."

"You had an intruder in your house last night and you didn't think to call me?"

"I was scared and shook up," Carly said defensively. "I called 9-1-1."

Joe was obviously mad at her. She didn't blame him. Listening to her own flimsy excuses, she realized how bad it sounded. "Joe, I'm so sorry. I've had so much going on ever since I moved in here. My brain just isn't acting right. Please forgive me?"

Joe turned to her and wrapped her in his arms. "Of course I forgive you. I know you've had a lot going on. It just didn't sit right with me when I saw you drive past the hardware store with Rick. You looked like you were having a great time with him. I was jealous."

Carly leaned into his embrace. "I'm the one who should be sorry. I never should have allowed him to drive me to town. I should have just driven myself. We're just friends. Nothing else." Who was she trying to convince? Him, or herself. Shaking the unwanted thought from her head, she pulled back to look up into Joe's face. "I have a lot to tell you."

"I'd like to hear it," he said.

She made sandwiches and poured them some iced tea.

Sitting across from him at the island, she told him everything that had happened after he left last night until he showed up at her door this afternoon.

When she had finished, she leaned back and waited for his reaction.

Joe mulled over everything she had told him before speaking. "So, you have a sister named Trinny and you think she's a ghost reaching out to you?"

"Yes," Carly said. "I believe she's the one I've been seeing."

"Carly, maybe this Trinny woman just skipped town. I've heard the rumors about her, too. That she took off with a bunch of your aunt's pricey items and skedaddled."

"Then who am I seeing? Whose haunting this place and why?" Carly demanded.

"I don't know, Carly," Joe said.

"I know you're having a hard time believing there's a ghost here, but I know what I saw. That's why tomorrow, I'm going to go see Madam Hornbeck."

Joe laughed, "You're kidding, right?"

"No, I'm not."

"You'll be wasting your time. She's a wacko who claims she can talk to the dead."

"I understand that," Carly said. "But I'm willing to listen to what she has to say."

Joe reached over and traced her cheek with his thumb. "Ok, baby, but please, just don't be dooped. She's just out for the money, is all."

Carly closed her eyes for a moment. When she opened them back up, she looked questioningly at Joe. "I wonder why Aunt Ruth insisted on staying here if she thought the place was haunted. Why didn't she just sell it and move somewhere else?"

"No idea," Joe said. "She used to tell people that she would never leave this place because this is where her treasure was."

"Her treasure? You mean, like her money or something?"

"No," Joe said. "I always got the impression that she had something hidden here that meant more to her than her money. What it was, no one knows. But from all the rumors that circulated about her, she swore she would never leave here because of her treasure."

"That's weird," Carly said. "She had this big house and all that money. What could be more valuable than that?"

Joe got a mischievous look on his face and he lowered his voice and squinted one eye. "Maybe it's a pirate's treasure worth a fortune. You know, diamonds, precious jewels and such." He said this using a pirate's voice and Carly laughed at him.

"Oohhhh, a treasure hunt! What fun!" she said, laughing.

Joe got up from his seat and started walking around the island toward her in a menacing way, "I'm going to get me some pirate's booty," he said.

Carly jumped up out of her seat and took off running down the hall, laughing so hard she couldn't catch her breath.

Joe caught her in the foyer and grabbed her around the waist.

Spinning her around to face him, he planted a hot, wet kiss on her lips. "I've got me the best treasure right here," he said.

Carly kissed him back in earnest. All thoughts of Rick erased from her mind.

Chapter 13

Carly woke to the sound of a storm. Thunder rumbled and lightning blazed paths across the sky. The gray clouds and heavy rain darkened her room and made the house feel dreary and cold.

Sitting up in bed, she looked around the room. She hadn't been awakened during the night by any strange noises or anyone calling her name.

In fact, she had slept like the dead.

Oh, nice analogy, she thought to herself.

Throwing off the covers, she swung her legs over the side of the bed and stood up.

Immediately, she noticed something wrong. Her foot had stepped in something gritty and slightly wet.

Looking down at the floor, she couldn't tell what she had stepped in. The room was cast in shadows due to the storm, so visibility was limited.

She hobbled over to the light switch trying not to get whatever it was she had stepped in, spread all over the floor.

Flipping on the light, she gasped.

Making a trail from the door to the side of the bed were footprints made of dirt and mud.

Carly leaned down and looked at one of the prints. It was a small footprint. Clearly a woman's. They were barefoot prints, too. She could clearly make out the narrow heel and toes shaped out of mud.

Throwing open the door that led into the hallway, she saw that the footprints continued on down the hall toward the stairs.

Following them, they led her down the stairs, across the foyer and to the front door.

Carly checked the alarm. It was still set. If someone had come into the house through the front door, the alarm should have gone off, alerting her to their presence.

But the alarm had not gone off.

She turned off the alarm, unlocked the door and stepped out onto the veranda.

The footprints led across the veranda and down the steps to the yard.

The sky was an ominous dark gray and rain poured down from the eves in torrents.

She poked her head out from under the roof over the veranda to see if she could see where the footprints went, but they seemed to disappear at the bottom of the steps.

Not wanting to get wet, she decided not to go down the steps to see which direction the footprints came from. The rain would have washed away any evidence of them anyway.

Not being dressed yet, she didn't relish the idea of Vernon spotting her in her nightgown. Goodness knows enough folks around here had already seen her in it, but she didn't want the number going up, so she hastily scanned the yard to make sure Vernon hadn't already seen her and made a hasty retreat back inside.

Grabbing a bucket from the laundry room, she filled it with some dish soap and water, then began cleaning up the footprints.

Starting at the front door, she scrubbed her way up to her bedroom. She used the vacuum cleaner on the area rug next to the bed to get the dirt up, then dumping the dirty water down the bathtub drain, she rinsed out the bucket and took it back to the laundry room.

It really creeped her out to know that someone had stood beside her bed while she was sleeping and watched her. How long had they stood there? Why didn't she wake up when they came into her room? How had someone gotten into the house without setting off the alarm? It was obviously a woman since the footprints were so small. Was it Trinny? Did ghosts leave footprints? Doubtful.

A shiver ran up her spine.

After getting dressed, she headed down to the kitchen for a quick breakfast.

Anxious to go see Madam Hornbeck, she opted for a small bowl of cereal and a cup of coffee.

While she ate her breakfast, she called Joe.

"Something weird happened here last night, Joe," she told him.

"Let me guess," he said. "Another intruder?" he chuckled, but when she didn't respond, he said, "I'm sorry, Carly. I was just joking. Tell me what happened."

"It was another intruder," she said flatly.

"Seriously?"

"Yeah, only this time they left muddy footprints from the front door all the way up to the side of my bed."

"What? Didn't the alarm go off?" Joe asked.

"No," Carly said. "I thought that was weird, too. I mean, if they came through the front door, wouldn't that have tripped it?"

"Maybe your friend, Rick, didn't install it properly and it doesn't work."

"We tried it out several times," Carly said, not missing the underlying nasty tone in Joe's voice.

"Well, maybe it needs to be tested again," Joe said. "I'll be over later today to take a look at it."

"Hey, another chance to see you?" Carly asked. "I'll take it."

She got off the phone and cleaned up her dishes.

Grabbing an umbrella from the coat closet, she headed out the door.

As she stepped out onto the veranda, she suddenly got the distinct feeling she was being watched. A creepy feeling tingled along her spine.

Looking out into the yard and gardens, she couldn't tell if anyone was out there or not.

With the rain pouring down as hard as it was, she could hardly see five feet in front of her.

Shrugging off the feeling, she popped the umbrella open, ran down the steps and dashed for her car.

Sliding into the driver's seat, she threw her purse onto the seat next to her and tossed the umbrella into the backseat. Turning the ignition over, the car purred to life.

As she switched on the defroster to defog the windows, she noticed something smeared on the windshield.

Carly reached up and rubbed the spots with the back of her hand, but they wouldn't come off. Leaning closer to get a better look, she realized they were words smeared in mud across the outside of her windshield. The letters spelled out, *HELP ME.*

Carly recoiled from the glass. How had the rain not removed it? As hard as it was raining, anything on the windshield should have been washed off.

She stared harder at the muddy words and realized they must have been put on really heavy in order for the rain not to have removed them...or they were an otherworldly message, in which rain could not wash them off.

Totally freaked out, Carly grabbed the umbrella from the backseat. Jumping from the car, she raced back to the house through the pouring rain.

Once inside, she gulped several lungfuls of air. Someone was definitely trying to reach out to her. There was no other explanation.

She felt around in her back pocket for her cell phone to call Joe and realized she had dropped it down into her purse which was still on the front passenger seat of the car.

"Gggrrr," she spat out through clenched teeth.

She seized the umbrella from where she had thrown it on the floor by the front door and stepped back out into the deluge of water pouring down from the sky.

Running as fast as she could to the car, she flung open the passenger side door and grabbed her purse off the seat. She stole a quick glance at the windshield again and shuddered.

Slamming the door shut, she turned to run back to the house, but stopped dead in her tracks. The umbrella slid from her trembling hands and hit the ground beside her, but she didn't notice.

Standing on the veranda was the ghostly form of a young woman with long, dark hair and sunken eyes, her ghost feet caked in mud. She slowly raised her arm and Carly could hear the words *help me* float to her over the pounding rain.

Carly couldn't breath. All she could do was stare at the pale, transparent form.

The ghost kept imploring her for help. She took a step toward Carly, but seemed reluctant to come any closer.

Carly watched in horror as the misty figure reached out her arm again and whispered, *help me Carly.*

She didn't know how long she stood there transfixed by the specter, but suddenly someone grabbed her arm, bringing her back to her senses.

"What's wrong with you?" Vernon growled in her ear. "You daft or something?"

Carly looked at Vernon, then pointed toward the veranda. "There," was all she was able to say.

Vernon turned his head toward the house and scanned the veranda. He turned back to Carly with a look of confusion on his old, wrinkled face. "What? What are you going on about?'

Carly looked back toward where the ghostly figure had been, but she was gone.

Sputtering, she looked helplessly at Vernon. "Did you see her? Did you see the ghost?"

Rain poured down in her eyes as she frantically searched the area for the apparition.

Vernon was looking at her like she had lost her mind. "What's wrong with you, girl? Are you mad? Ghost? Bah, you're just plum crazy, you are."

Vernon picked up the umbrella, holding it over her head as he escorted her back to the house.

When they got to the veranda, Carly hesitated, looking around, but Vernon place his hand firmly on her lower back and shoved.

"Get going, missy," he shouted to her over the noise of the storm. "It's pouring down the rain, if you haven't noticed."

Carly opened the front door and Vernon, with his hand still on her back, pushed her over the threshold.

"Look at you," he scolded her. "Soaking wet like you don't have the brains God gave a goose."

Carly looked down at her drenched clothes, then over at Vernon. He was just as soaked as she was.

"Mr. Knowles, I'm sorry," she told him, taking in his pitiful appearance.

"What were you doing out there? Trying to catch your death of pneumonia?"

"No, I was on my way to see someone, when..." she stopped without completing the sentence.

"When what?" Vernon demanded. "You decided to play in the rain or something?"

"Didn't you see her?" Carly asked. "She was standing on the veranda in front of the door."

"See who? All I saw was you standing in the rain staring up at the house. You just stood there like you were in some kind of trance, or something. I figured I'd better go out and see what was the matter with you."

Carly wasn't going to try to convince Vernon of what she had seen. No one believed her. No one believed she was seeing the ghost of her half sister.

"Thank you, Mr. Knowles," she said, instead. "I appreciate you coming out to check on me."

"Don't take it to mean I like you or anything," Vernon said. "I just didn't think the new owner of my home needed to be out there standing like a statue in the rain."

Without thinking, Carly leaned over and gave Vernon a quick hug.

"Hey now," he said, stepping back. "No need for that."

"Let me get you a towel," Carly said. "Do you want a cup of hot coffee?"

Vernon shrugged his shoulders and said just loud enough for her to hear him, "Well, sure, fine. I guess that would be ok."

Carly brought them both a towel out of the bathroom, then put on a pot of coffee.

As they sat wrapped in their towels and sipping the hot beverage, Carly looked closely at Vernon.

Guessing he was probably around seventy or so, she surmised that in his younger days, he must have been a rather good looking man.

Where his hair was now gray, she figured it had probably been brown in his youth. His slightly stooped frame at one time had probably been tall and muscular.

Intrigued with this man, she set her cup down and asked, "Mr. Knowles, what brought you to Montgomery Manor?"

"Work," he said. "What normally brings someone to a plantation if he doesn't own it?"

"You told me you started here when you were fifteen. Why have you stayed all these years? Were you ever married? Do you have any kids?" The questions tumbled out of her, one after the other.

Vernon looked like he was going to snub off her questions, but instead, took a deep breath and said, "I stayed because it was easy work and good pay for someone of my station. Didn't figure I could do any better anywhere else." He took a sip of coffee and continued, "No, I never married. Oh, I wanted to, but it just never happened. And since I was never married, I never had any children."

Carly watched him for a moment. "Thank you, Mr. Knowles. I appreciate you talking to me."

"Call me Vernon," he said. "If you're going to be sticking around for awhile, we may as well call each other by our given names."

Carly reached out and gently squeezed his hand that he had laying on the counter. He didn't pull away.

"Thank you," she said, earnestly.

"I best be getting home and getting out of these wet clothes before I catch a chill," Vernon said, slipping off the bar stool.

"Take my umbrella," Carly said. "No need in you getting any wetter."

She walked him to the door and watched him trudge out across the yard and around the corner to the carriage house.

A warmth spread through her at the thought of him. He was finally warming up to her a bit. Oh, he was still grumpy and unpleasant for the most part, but she was wearing him down.

She closed the door and made her way back to the kitchen, grabbing her purse off the floor by the doorway on her way through.

It was soaked through from having hung on her arm as she stood watching the ghost. She turned it upside down and dumped the contents of it onto the island.

Riffling around through the items that lay there, she found her phone and punched in Joe's number. The phone just rang and rang, finally going to voicemail.

She noticed it was close to 10:00 a.m.

She really wanted to go see Madam Hornbeck, but the thought of climbing back into her car with that message smeared all over it, made her think twice.

Maybe she should wait till the rain stopped so she could properly clean the mud off the windshield.

No, she really wanted to go talk to Madam Hornbeck now. If she kept having these incidents with the ghost and didn't know what she should do or how she should handle it, she'd go crazy. Obviously, the ghost wasn't just going to go away.

Her mind made up, she called Rick.

Chapter 14

Carly waited on the veranda for Rick to show up.

When she had called him, he told her he would be there shortly. It had already been almost fifteen minutes.

Feeling antsy and anxious, she paced back and forth, wringing her hands. She kept jerking her head from side to side in case the ghost showed up again. She had left the front door cracked open in case she had to make a hasty retreat.

The storm was slowing down. Black clouds still blanketed the sky, but the rain had slowed to a gentle drizzle.

Carly wiped beads of sweat off her forehead as the passing storm left a pressing humidity in it's wake.

She turned to make another lap around the veranda when she heard the rumble of Rick's pickup trudging up her drive.

He pulled up next to her car and got out.

The look on his face gave Carly the impression he wasn't happy to be there.

He stepped up onto the veranda as she rushed over to him.

"Rick," she said, almost breathless. "Thank you for coming."

"What happened?" he asked. "You sounded scared on the phone."

"Someone wrote on my car's windshield," Carly explained. "In mud."

"You called me over here because someone put mud on your car?"

"Not just mud," Carly said. "Words in mud."

"Why didn't you call Joe?" Rick asked, sounding slightly irritated. "I'm sure he would have rushed to your rescue."

"I called him, but it just went to voicemail," she said, sheepishly.

Rick looked hard at her for a moment, then scratched his chin. "You know," he said. "I'm not a *last option* kind of guy. I don't take second fiddle to anyone."

"What?" Carly asked. "I never said you did." She was confused by his attitude and a little hurt that he would accuse her of this.

"It's obvious you're in a relationship with Joe. So, why call me? Was it because he was unavailable, so you thought I'd do instead?"

"No, Rick," Carly said, affronted. "I thought we were friends."

"I'm not going to be used, Carly."

"I'm not using you, Rick."

"What do you call it, then?"

Carly stared dumbfounded at him. What happened here? She had such a good time with him before. Why was he acting this way now?

"Carly, from now on if you need something, maybe you'd better just call Joe."

"Rick, what's going on?" Carly asked.

"I thought you and me were going on," Rick said. "That is until I brought you home yesterday. It was very clear Joe was jealous. He would only have been that jealous if the two of you had something going on. I don't want to get in the middle of that."

"Rick, I didn't mean to put you in the middle," Carly said. "I had a great time with you yesterday. I thought we were just friends, though. I never meant to insinuate anything else."

"I guess I got the signals crossed, then," Rick said.

"I guess you did," Carly said, her anger rising.

"Then call Joe from now on if you need something," Rick huffed as he walked back down the steps.

"Rick, wait," Carly called to him. "Please."

"What, Carly?" he demanded. "What do you need?"

"I need you to check my car. I need you to help me clean it off."

Rick walked over and looked at the windshield of her car. He traced his finger through the muddy words.

Looking closely at his finger, he turned to her and lifted his finger in the air for her to see.

"It's mud," he said, flatly. "Just get a rag and wipe it off."

Wiping his muddy finger across the leg of his jeans, he crawled back into his pickup and drove off. He never looked back at her once.

Carly stood on the veranda and watched him drive away, a heaviness in her heart. Why did she feel like she just lost the best friend she would ever have? Why did it feel like her heart was breaking? She didn't like the way things ended with Rick. She knew she would miss his easy banter and his teasing.

Stomping her foot in frustration, she turned on her heel and went inside in search of a rag.

She pulled the bucket out of the laundry room again and filled it with soap and water. Grabbing an old dishrag, she lifted the bucket and headed out to her car.

The sky still promised more rain, but for now, she was given a reprieve. Tiny droplets of water fell from the sky, but not enough to soak her through.

She set the bucket down on the ground next to the car and lifted the sopping, soapy rag out of the water and slapped it onto the windshield.

Rubbing as briskly as she could, she cleaned the mud off the windshield. Streaks of dirty water ran down the hood of the car and puddled on the ground in front of it.

Assessing her cleaning job, she dumped the bucket out onto the ground and returned the rag and bucket to the laundry room.

She still couldn't believe the way Rick had acted. He was hoping for a relationship with her? He sure didn't act like it, always poking fun at her and teasing her. More often than not, she wanted to wring his neck. But, if she was honest with herself, she rather enjoyed his bantering and teasing. She spent a lot of time in his company laughing. There was something about him that made her feel at home, comfortable, at ease. But she really liked Joe, too. He was gorgeous, fun and kissed really well. *I wonder what Rick kisses like,* she thought to herself.

Shaking the thoughts from her head, She quickly changed into clean, dry clothes, checked the alarm, grabbed her purse and headed for the car.

Sliding behind the wheel, she sat in the stuffy, hot car for a moment before she started the engine. This day was not turning out the way she would have liked. She hoped things at Madam Hornbeck's would go a little better.

~~~

The small pink house with the white shutters was easy to find. It sat close to the road and was surrounded by a neat, white picket fence. A large yellow sign hanging in the front yard read, *Madam Hornbeck's Mystical Magic*.

The stone walkway up to the door was lined with colorful flowers and a palm with a large eye in the middle of it was painted onto the large glass window next to the front door.

Hesitating only momentarily, Carly stepped up to the door and knocked.

A lyrical voice floated to her through the closed door, "Come in."

Carly turned the knob and stepped into a room that was lit only by candlelight. Along the wall next to the door, shelves were full of crystals of all colors, salt lamps and incense burners. On the back wall, assorted necklaces, bracelets and earrings were hung from pegs and spinning towers. Soft, white, fluffy rugs were placed around the room, offering a softness to the atmosphere. A strong incense was burning in a long wooden holder, clouding the room with a hazy fog. She held in a cough that threatened from the pungent smell and made her way toward a desk in the back of the room where a lady in a light blue, gauzy wrap was waiting for her.

"Hello and welcome," the lady said. "I'm Madam Hornbeck." She held out her hand for Carly to shake.

Carly gently took the woman's hand in her own and gave it a short, quick shake. "I'm Carly Montgomery. Nice to meet you."

The woman drew in a sharp intake of breath and squeezed Carly's hand, not letting it go.

"You, my dear, are not alone," she said in a feathery, wispy voice, looking over Carly's shoulder.

Carly tried to withdraw her hand, but Madam Hornbeck had a strong grip on it.

Carly stared, wide-eyed at the woman while taking in her odd appearance.

She was middle aged, probably around fifty, with long, dark hair twisted back into a braid that was adorned with colorful strings and beads. A gauzy scarf was wrapped tightly, but neatly, around her forehead and hung to her waist. Heavy makeup was packed around her eyes and across her cheeks and a weighty, floral scent surrounded her. Bracelets of many colors dangled from her arms and every finger had a ring on it. Carly noticed a necklace around her long, sculpted neck that held a pear shaped emerald stone.

"Did you hear me, dear?" Madam Hornbeck asked her.

"Y...y...yes," Carly stammered.

"You already know, don't you?" Madam Hornbeck asked, giving her a deep look.

"That's why I'm here."

"Come, let's get started," Madam Hornbeck said, leading Carly around the desk and behind a beaded curtain that blocked off the front room from the reading room.

The small, claustrophobic room was dark, except for a single candle perched in the middle of a circular table that was covered with a white gauzy cloth. Only two chairs were present, one on either side of the table.

A soft, pleasant smelling incense was burning in this room and the smoke from it was making Carly feel relaxed and slightly intoxicated.

The room was too dark to take in much more of the décor, so Carly slid into the chair offered to her and sat back, enjoying the peacefulness of the room.

Madam Hornbeck eased herself into her chair and clasped her hands in front of her on the table.

"Tell me what you've seen," she said to Carly in a low, musical tone.

Carly's head was beginning to feel like it was in a fog, but it was a peaceful, relaxing fog.

"I've seen a ghost in my house," she said, almost dreamily.

"Indeed. Go on," coaxed Madam Hornbeck.

"I've seen her in mirrors and out in the graveyard."

"Tell me about this ghost. What does she look like."

"She looks like me," Carly said, slowly. Her mind was getting fuzzy and she was beginning to get a bit drowsy from the incense.

"Indeed," Madam Hornbeck said. "Go on."

"I think it's my sister...well, half sister," Carly said.

"Let me see your hands, my dear."

Carly held out her hands to her, palms up.

Madam Hornbeck stretched out Carly's right hand and traced a path along the inside of the palm with her finger.

"Trinny...," Madam Hornbeck said.

Carly's mind was instantly clear and she gasped. "Yes, I think it's Trinny!"

"You are right. It is your sister, Trinny. She was with you when you came into my shop. She was standing behind you on the left."

"So, you can see her? Now?" Carly asked, excitedly, scanning the room for the familiar misty form.

"Yes, she's here with us now."

"What does she want?" Carly asked.

"That's what you need to find out," Madam Hornbeck said.

"How?" Carly asked, frustrated.

"Tell me what all has happened since she first showed herself to you."

Carly told her of seeing Trinny in the mirrors, in the cemetery, on the veranda. She explained about the muddy footprints and the words written in mud on her windshield.

"Her spirit is getting stronger," Madam Hornbeck said. "She is reaching out to you, Carly. Reaching out, needing your help."

"What can I do?"

"You must not be afraid of her. She is not here to hurt you. She only wants to communicate with you."

"How did she leave mud on my windshield that the rain wouldn't wash off?"

Madam Hornbeck looked over Carly's shoulder and raised her eyebrows in a questioning manner. "Trinny said she mixed some of her essence into the mud so it would not wash off with the rain."

Carly swung her head around and looked over her shoulder, but she didn't see Trinny standing there. "Why can't I see her now?"

"She is here in spirit, but is saving her energy to be able to communicate with you later," Madam Hornbeck told her. "She can only use so much energy at a time. If she uses it all now to appear to us, she won't be able to use any later until she goes into the gray and rests for awhile. She hears us and knows what we are talking about and is anxious to communicate with you."

"Into the gray? What does that mean?" Carly asked.

"It's a place that spirits go to rest."

"Why doesn't she communicate with me now?"

"What she has to tell you is for you, and you alone. It is not for my eyes or ears."

"How do I communicate with her?"

"When she appears to you, talk to her. If her spirit is strong enough, she will be able to talk back."

"Will I be able to hear her?" Carly asked. "Anytime I've seen her, I've only seen her mouth move."

"As her spirit gets stronger, she will be able to speak to you and you will be able to hear her."

"I'm afraid, Madam Hornbeck," Carly said. "I've never talked to a ghost before."

"It's perfectly normal to be afraid the first time. If you weren't, I would think something was wrong with you."

Madam Hornbeck gently squeezed Carly's hands. "As far as the other matter goes," she said with a wink. "Your heart will guide you in the right direction. Don't fight it."

Carly stared, open mouthed at Madam Hornbeck. "How did you know...?"

"I see all things, my dear."

"You didn't use a crystal ball or Tarot cards, though," Carly said.

"Smoke and mirrors, my dear," Madam Hornbeck answered her. "Someone who truly has the gift, has no need of such things."

"Thank you so much, Madam Hornbeck," Carly said, getting up to leave. "You don't know how much I appreciate your help."

"You come back anytime you need my help," Madam Hornbeck said. "I see good things in you, my dear."

Carly walked out into the front room and began to dig around in her purse for her wallet. "How much do I owe you?"

"On the house, my dear."

"Are you sure?" Carly asked.

"Indeed, I am," Madam Hornbeck said. "I'm just glad I am able to help you...and Trinny."

Carly looked around the room, but still didn't see her sister's ghostly form anywhere.

"Madam Hornbeck?" she asked. "Is Trinny with me all the time?"

"Only when she wants to be."

"How will I know?" Carly asked.

"You'll learn to feel her presence when she is around."

Carly simply nodded and turned and walked out the door.

"Trinny," she said, softly so no one would hear her. "If you're with me, it's ok. I'm glad you are."

Carly could have sworn she felt a soft touch brush against her cheek. She lifted her hand and gently touched the spot.

A warm smile spread across her lips.

From this point on, she would no longer
be afraid of the ghost that was her sister.

Chapter 15

Carly pulled into her drive just as her cell phone rang. Digging it out of her purse, she saw that it was Joe.

She quickly threw the car into park, turned off the ignition and jumped out.

"Joe," she said, excitedly. "I'm glad you called."

"I saw you tried calling earlier, but I missed it," he said. "Everything ok?"

"I have a lot to tell you," Carly said, almost breathless with excitement. "When are you coming over?"

"Let me get cleaned up and I'll be right over. Say in about an hour?"

"Great. I'll fix us something to eat while I'm waiting on you."

Carly hung up and dashed up the front steps of the mansion. She searched the veranda for any sign of Trinny, but no ghostly form or mist appeared.

The sky was beginning to darken to a steel gray, and Carly knew it wouldn't be long till the clouds opened up and dumped a ton of rain on them again.

Rushing inside, she scrambled around trying to find something to fix for dinner. Settling on baked Salmon over rice and a side salad, she got to work getting everything ready while anxiously waiting for Joe to show up.

As she chopped up the vegetables for the salad, she kept glancing around the kitchen for any sign that Trinny might be present.

Nothing.

Was she here? Or in the gray recharging herself? Carly kept going over in her head everything that Madam Hornbeck had told her. She would be able to communicate with her sister. That only meant one thing, though. Trinny was, indeed, dead. What happened to her? Where was she? Why did she just up and leave Aunt Ruth and take all that valuable stuff with her? She was hoping to get all these answers and more once she learned how to properly communicate with her sister.

Suddenly, a thought crossed her mind. Would she still be scared when Trinny appeared to her or spoke to her? She couldn't help but think she would still be a little frightened about it. It wasn't everyday someone spoke to a ghost, especially her.

Carly sucked in a deep breath and blew it out slowly through pursed lips. *Relax*, she told herself. *She's your sister. She doesn't want to scare you or hurt you. She only wants to talk to you.*

Joe showed up just as the fish was coming out of the oven.

Carly was so glad to see him, she flew across the room and launched herself into his arms.

"Whoa there," he said, laughing.

"Sorry," Carly said. "I'm just so excited to see you."

"Glad to hear it. Now what's all this stuff you have to tell me about?"

"Let me get our plates fixed, then I'll tell you."

Carly fixed their plates, then pulled up her stool to the island and told him about the muddy footprints on the floor, the mud caked words on the windshield and her visit to Madam Hornbeck's.

"So let me get this straight," Joe said. "Madam Hornbeck told you that you're being haunted by your sister, Trinny, and that she's reaching out to you and trying to communicate with you."

"Yes!" Carly said, excitedly. "She's who I've been seeing in the mirror and she's the one I saw in the graveyard. She's trying to reach out to me."

"But why?" Joe asked. "Why would she be reaching out to you?"

"I have no idea. That's why the next time she tries to communicate with me, I need to try to let her come through instead of running like a scaredy cat."

"Carly, I don't know," Joe said, skeptically. "This all sounds like a load of hogwash to me."

"That's because you've never seen her," Carly said. "Maybe if you did, you'd believe me."

"Maybe," Joe said. Carly heard the doubt in his voice, but she pushed on.

"Joe, I think she's the one who left the muddy footprints last night."

"You're kidding, right? Ghosts can't leave footprints."

"Sure they can. I've been looking up ghost stuff online and I've found a few Youtube videos on the subject," Carly said. "Have you ever heard about people sprinkling baby powder on the floor in suspected ghost cases to see if the ghost leaves any tracks behind? Tons of cases have shown that the ghosts do, in fact, sometimes leave their prints in the powder."

Joe stared at her blankly for a moment, then shook his head and laughed. "That's probably where you went wrong, watching videos online about it."

"Joe, it's real," Carly insisted. "Ghost hunters have captured EVPs, shadow figures, phantom footsteps and even the rare image of a ghost on their equipment. Why is it so hard to imagine that they might also leave footprints behind?"

"Because frankly, Carly, I don't believe in ghosts."

"I didn't use to," Carly said. "But seeing is believing."

"Well, I've never seen one," Joe said.

"I hadn't either until I moved here," Carly said. "If you hang around long enough, you just might see her, too."

"Speaking of hanging around, don't let me forget to check the alarm system," Joe said, changing the subject.

Carly let the topic drop for now, but knew it was far from over.

They finished eating their dinner and Joe helped her clean up the kitchen.

As they walked out to the front door, Carly stopped Joe by touching his arm. "I'm not sure the alarm was the problem."

"What do you mean?" Joe asked.

"If it was Trinny who left the footprints, then that may be why the alarm wasn't tripped. Maybe ghosts don't set off security systems."

"Carly," Joe said, sounding a bit exasperated. "If someone left muddy tracks on your floors, then that someone is alive and kicking. Not some ghost stomping through the house."

"Whatever," Carly said, cheerfully. She knew ghosts were real and she knew in her heart who left the tracks on her floor. She just smiled to herself as Joe checked out the security system.

"Everything seems to be working just fine," Joe said, perplexed. "Still seems weird that if someone came through the front door, they would have tripped the alarm. Maybe you should still call Rick to come check this thing out. Maybe I'm missing something."

"You want me to call Rick?" Carly asked, stunned. "After the way you acted last time I called him?"

"I'm not going to say I like the idea of you calling him, but he installed this thing, so let him check it out and make sure it really is working correctly."

"Maybe later," Carly said, stalling. She couldn't help but think that after her conversation with Rick earlier, he probably wouldn't come anyway.

It was now mid afternoon and an impending storm was brewing on the horizon. Dark clouds were building and what little sun was visible was getting blotted out by the darkening masses.

Carly and Joe sat on the veranda and watched as the humidity in the air brought a bank of fog up out of the earth and covered the ground like a blanket.

Neither of them said anything, as they sat in silence, holding hands and watching as lightening sent streaks across the sky and thunder rumbled off in the distance.

"That sky is going to open up and dump heaps on us shortly," Joe said, breaking the companionable silence.

"Seems so," Carly said. "Want to take a walk before it hits?"

"Sure," Joe said, getting to his feet, pulling her up with him.

"Let's walk down to the bridge," Carly suggested. "It's so peaceful there and we should be able to make it there and back before the rain hits."

Joe looked up at the darkening sky and nodded his head. "Yeah, we should be ok. Rain shouldn't be here for a little while yet."

He grabbed her hand and they stepped off the veranda and followed the stone path around to the back of the house.

As they passed the carriage house, Carly saw that Vernon's lights were on. She thought about stopping and asking if he wanted to join them, but decided she wanted Joe all to herself, so she pushed the idea out of her head and they strolled on past and up the hill toward the cemetery.

The thick layer of fog that covered the ground was as high as their knees as they walked past the old forgotten gravestones, now barely visible. It swirled around their legs as they moved through it, creating a billowing effect along the ground.

Carly glanced over at Rutherford Montgomery's tall marker stone as they passed and wondered why she was continually drawn to it. Sure, it was big and tall and impressive, but somehow she didn't think that was the reason. She tore her eyes away from it as Joe led her farther back through the graves toward the river.

Small drops of rain had just begun to fall when they reached the rope bridge. Heavy fog hovered over the water and swirled around in an eerie dance.

Carly walked to the center of the bridge, looking out over the river, mesmerized by the fog in it's mystifying crawl across the water.

Joe walked up behind her and wrapped his arms around her waist. Nuzzling her hair, he whispered, "We'd better be heading back. This rain is going to pick up before long and we're going to get soaked."

Carly leaned back into his arms and savored the moment of feeling him so close to her. His cologne, mingled with the scent of the impending rain, filled her senses making her a little lightheaded. She turned in his arms and allowed him to kiss her deeply before they headed back up the path toward the cemetery.

Hand in hand, they stepped out of the small cluster of trees as the rain began to come down a little harder.

The wind was beginning to pick up and the fog was rising up off the ground, creating wispy clouds that danced along the tops of the gravestones.

As they walked farther into the cemetery, Carly glanced at Rutherford Montgomery's stone and froze. Standing next to the grave, the ghost of Trinny was watching them as they came nearer.

Carly squeezed Joe's hand and nodded toward the grave.

"What?" Joe asked. "What is it?"

"There. By the gravestone," Carly whispered. "It's Trinny."

Joe looked in the direction that Carly was pointing, then looked down at her in surprise. "What are you talking about? I don't see anyone."

Carly looked quickly at Joe, then back at Trinny. How could he not see her. She was standing right there.

Suddenly, Trinny's eyes turned black, her face twisting into a horrid, angry expression and she let out a shriek that cut through the air, piercing Carly's ears. Raising her hands up and curling her fingers into claws, she flew across the graveyard toward Joe and Carly.

Carly let out a scream and ducked just as Trinny sliced through the air between her and Joe, breaking their hands apart.

Carly scrambled to stay on her feet and took off running. She could hear Joe calling for her to stop.

When she reached the bottom of the hill, she turned frantically around looking to see where Joe was.

She saw him cresting the hill and letting out the breath she was holding, ran over to meet him.

"Carly, what in the world…,?" Joe asked her, looking at her like she'd lost her mind. "What happened back there?"

Carly stared at him dumbfounded. "What do you mean, what happened? Didn't you see her? Didn't you hear her scream?"

Joe took Carly by the shoulders to steady her. "Carly, I didn't see anyone, but you. And you were the only one who screamed."

"I saw Trinny, Joe," Carly demanded. "She was standing by Rutherford's grave and then...she suddenly...turned angry and yelled...and then flew at us. I had to duck to keep her from colliding with me. Didn't you feel anything when she ripped our hands apart?"

"You're the one who jerked your hand out of mine and screamed."

Carly just shook her head and turned back toward the house.

She saw the curtains at Vernon's kitchen window flutter closed and knew he had just witnessed their argument. She didn't care. She stormed off toward the house just as the clouds above broke loose and poured rain down on them.

Joe caught up to her on the veranda. He grabbed her arm to stop her from rushing into the house and swung her around to face him. "Carly, there was no one there, but you and me," he said softly. "The fog was swirling around and rising up from the ground. It was probably just an illusion of the wind and fog mixed that made it look like a person standing there. As for the scream you thought you heard, it was probably just the wind whistling past some of the old gravestones. It's a little scary in a cemetery when there's a storm. But I assure, we were alone."

"I did not imagine anything. Trinny was there. She was angry. She screamed. I ran. End of story."

Joe grabbed Carly and wrapped his arms around her tight, pulling her up against his body as if shielding her from something. "No one is out there trying to get you, Carly. I promise you."

Carly let him hold her for a long time. She wasn't going to argue with him anymore. If he didn't want to believe her, then fine. But she knew what she saw. What she heard.

Why was Trinny suddenly so angry? Why had she tried to plow her over? Madam Hornbeck told her Trinny didn't want to hurt her, only talk to her. Well, that certainly didn't seem like she wanted to talk. That was a threat and Carly wasn't taking it lightly. A shiver ran up her spine at the image of Trinny rushing at her that way. Seems she needed to be afraid of the ghost after all.

Joe didn't stick around for long after they got back to the house.

They sat on the veranda drinking some coffee Carly had brewed, but once she was relaxed and calmed down, he took their cups back inside and came back out, but didn't take his seat. "I'm going to head home and give you some time to yourself. You've had a rough day and need to rest."

Carly looked up at him trying to gauge his words, but all she saw was genuine concern in his eyes.

"It has been a long day," she said. "I'm a bit confused, but I really don't want to talk about it. I just need to sort some stuff out in my head, I guess."

Joe leaned over and gave her a quick kiss on her cheek. "Don't forget to call Rick and have him come check out that alarm system."

Carly only nodded.

After Joe left, Carly picked up her phone to call Rick, but thought better of it. She knew he would be angry that she called him to come fix another problem, so she put her phone back in her pocket and headed inside.

She knew there was nothing wrong with the security system anyway. Both Rick and Joe had checked it out and it worked perfect every time. Ghosts apparently couldn't set it off, so there was no use calling Rick to come check it out again. If it had been a real, live person who had come into her house, the alarm would have went off, but Trinny wasn't going to be able to set it off in her ghostly form, so checking it out a third time wasn't going to help the matter.

It was still early, but Carly was mentally exhausted. It truly had been a long day. The muddy footprints. The muddy windshield. The visit to Madam Hornbeck's. The attack in the cemetery. Then, finally, the argument with Joe. She had had enough for one day, so she carried herself up to her room and drew herself a hot bath. After which, she curled up in bed with a book and prayed for morning to come quickly.

Chapter 16

Carly woke up with a slight headache. Strange dreams and nightmarish images of Trinny plagued her all night.

Tossing the covers off, she slipped out of bed and got dressed.

She didn't bother looking around the room for any evidence that someone might have been there. She had spent most of the night tossing and turning and was sure that if someone had been there, she probably would have scared them off.

Feeling irritated and a little on edge, she brewed herself a pot of coffee and threw some bread in the toaster. She wasn't necessarily hungry this morning, but she knew she would probably feel better with a little something in her stomach. She hadn't eaten anything after her meal with Joe the day before and wondered if that might be the cause for the headache that was still pounding in her head.

Popping some Tylenol, she sipped her coffee and nibbled on her toast.

She knew what she had to do today. She knew she had to get answers for what happened with Trinny in the cemetery yesterday.

She was just getting ready to grab her purse and keys when the doorbell sounded.

Thinking it was Joe, she bolted for the door and swung it open.

Vernon stood in the doorway looking at her, his usual look of irritation on his face.

"Oh," Carly said. "Good morning, Vernon."

"Morning, missy," Vernon said, stepping past her into the foyer.

"Something I can do for you today?" she asked him.

"No, not really. I...uh...was just wondering if you were ok," he said, gruffly. "I couldn't help, but hear the argument between you and that fellow yesterday afternoon. You seemed rather upset."

"I'm sorry about that, Vernon," Carly said. "I'm fine, though."

"Well, next time you want to argue, do it somewhere besides right outside my window."

Carly couldn't help but laugh. "I'll make sure we do it somewhere you can't hear."

Vernon relaxed and gave her a tight smile. "Is that coffee I smell?"

Carly invited him to the kitchen for a cup of coffee, pouring herself another one as well. She figured she might need the extra caffeine anyway.

"Carly," Vernon said. "You want to tell me what all the fussing between you and Joe was all about?"

"It's really none...I mean...it's not important," Carly said. She had been about to tell him it was none of his business, but she was finally beginning to break through his shell and didn't want to slide backward. "We just had a difference of opinion on something."

"Looked like you'd seen a ghost, as white as you were," he said. His tone was more of a question than a statement.

Carly stared at him for a moment, not sure how to proceed, but throwing caution to the wind, she asked, "You've seen her too, haven't you?"

Vernon took a long drink of his coffee and smacked his lips before answering her. "You know, your aunt used to see her, too."

"So I've heard," Carly said. "Have *you* seen her?"

"I might have, on occasion."

"Why can't Joe see her?" Carly asked.

"Didn't know he couldn't."

"Did you know she was my half sister?"

"Yep."

"Why didn't you tell me before, then?" Carly asked.

"Wasn't sure I could trust you," Vernon said.

"What about now?" Carly asked.

"Not saying I trust you yet, but you're entitled to know, I guess."

"Know what?"

"That she's your half sister."

"I know that. I know she's my half sister."

"Well, then. There you go."

Carly just shook her head and laughed. "Vernon, you're just a ball of information, aren't you?"

"Some things it's just best to figure out on your own."

"If I ask you questions, will you answer them, since you obviously won't just spill your guts?"

"I'll answer what needs answering."

"Ok, fine," Carly said. "Why is she haunting me?"

"I have no idea."

"Why was she haunting my aunt?"

"I have no idea."

"What do you know?" Carly asked.

"Not much, I guess."

Talking to Vernon was like pulling teeth. She had to laugh, though. He was such a stubborn old man, but Carly couldn't help but like him.

"I have an errand to run in town," she said, getting to her feet. "Do you want anything while I'm there?"

Vernon set his cup down and slid off the bar stool. Scratching his head for a moment, he said, "No, don't reckon I do, but thanks for asking."

Carly walked with him out to the front door and opened it for him. "If you ever want to tell me something, Vernon, please don't hesitate. I need to learn as much as I can about this place, my aunt and about Trinny. If there's anything that you can share with me, I'd really appreciate it."

"If I have something to tell you, I'll tell you, missy," Vernon said, stepping out onto the veranda. "One word of caution, though. Don't make Trinny mad. She can get ugly when she's mad."

Carly watched Vernon hobble down the steps and around the side of the house before she closed the door and locked it behind her.

That man knows more than he's saying, she thought.

She jumped in her car and headed into town.

~~~

The small pink house with the white shudders came into view as Carly rounded the bend.

Pulling up in front of the house, she quickly threw the car into park and hopped out.

She hoped Madam Hornbeck was in today. If not, she didn't know what she would do, but thankfully, when she tried the doorknob, it turned in her hand and she stepped into the smoky, overly incensed front room of the shop.

Madam Hornbeck wasn't at the desk, so Carly walked back and pushed the beaded curtain aside and sticking her head in, called out for her.

Immediately, she knew she had made a mistake. Madam Hornbeck was seated at the small table across from a young woman. Both were surprised to see her pop her head into the room.

"Oh, I'm so sorry," Carly said, as she quickly backed out of the room.

Madam Hornbeck got out of her chair and came out into the front room. "Carly," she said, gently, but firmly. "You can't just barge into the room when I'm in a session. Please, have a seat and I'll be with you shortly." She indicated a small, fuzzy chair that was at the end of one of the bookcases.

Carly apologized again and went over and sat in the chair to wait.

Long minutes passed and she was starting to get impatient. She was still irritable and agitated from not sleeping well, combined with the fact that her mind kept replaying the events of yesterday.

Finally, she couldn't sit still any longer and got up to examine the different items around the room.

Finding a bowl of polished rocks, she began picking them up one at a time.

"Do you know what those are?" came Madam Hornbeck's musical voice from behind her.

Carly almost dropped the stone she was holding and turned around. She hadn't heard Madam Hornbeck come up behind her.

"Rocks?" Carly asked. "Pretty shiny rocks?"

Madam Hornbeck laughed and gently took the stone from her and turned it over in her hand. "This one is Rose Quartz. The Love Stone."

"Oh," Carly said, taking the rock back from Madam Hornbeck and placing it back in the bowl. "Do you have one that will allow me to communicate with Trinny? Something went wrong yesterday."

"You would want Quartz for that, too, my dear, just a different one, like Amethyst, perhaps," Madam Hornbeck said. "But first, come on back and let's talk about why you're here."

Carly followed her back to the room behind the beaded curtain. She looked around for the young woman that had been there earlier, but she was gone.

"I'm sorry about interrupting your session earlier. I didn't realize you had someone back here with you," Carly told her.

"It's always best to allow me to come out to you when you enter my shop. You never know when I might be in with someone. But no worries, my dear. She's a frequent visitor who is lost and needs help finding her way to the other side."

"Wait...you mean...she was a ghost?" Carly asked, shocked.

"Not all my clients are of this world. I help both the living and the dead," Madam Hornbeck told her.

No wonder Carly hadn't heard the girl leave. She had slipped out without a sound and simply vanished. Carly's curiosity wanted to ask Madam Hornbeck what had happened to the girl, but good manners kept her from inquiring. Instead, she focused on why she was here.

Taking a seat opposite Madam Hornbeck, Carly dived right in.

"I saw Trinny again yesterday," she said.

"Did you speak with her?"

"No," Carly said. "I was walking through the cemetery with my friend and I saw her appear next to one of my ancestor's gravestones. At first, she just seemed to be watching us, but then, her face turned all angry and she rushed at us and flew between us."

"Hhhmmm, I see," said Madam Hornbeck. "What happened then?"

"I ran."

"Did you see Trinny again after that?"

"No."

"I see," said Madam Hornbeck. "Did anything else happen during this encounter?"

"Yeah," Carly said. "Trinny screamed. Loud. It was so loud it hurt my ears. It was actually more like a shriek."

"Hhhmmm. What did your friend do during all this?"

"He claims he never saw, nor heard her."

"Indeed," Madam Hornbeck said, rubbing her chin. "If that is the case, then it was because Trinny chose for him not to see her. Spirits can pick and choose whom they appear to, and for some reason, Trinny didn't want to show herself to your friend."

"But why?" Carly asked. "And why was she so mad? She really frightened me."

"I do not know, my dear. These are things you will need to find out from her."

"But I'm afraid of her now. You should have seen her face. And she charged me. She tried to hurt me."

"No, my dear," Madam Hornbeck said. "She was not trying to hurt you. She was trying to warn you or protect you."

She has a funny way of showing it," Carly said.

"She would have had to have used up a lot of energy to appear, shriek at you and then rush you that way. She wouldn't use up all her energy for something like that unless she was trying very hard to warn you of something. Could there have been a wild animal around, or a predator of any kind?"

"No, I don't think so," Carly said. "It was late afternoon and it was just beginning to rain. My friend and I were heading back to the house. Nothing stands out as a threat or anything."

"Carly, do not be afraid of her," Madam Hornbeck said. "When she was here with you, I didn't notice any evil in her at all. Only goodness. Trust me when I tell you, she is only interested in your well being. She wants to communicate with you. Let her in."

"What if she attacks me again?"

Madam Hornbeck reached over and gently took Carly's hands in hers and squeezed. "Carly, she was not attacking you. If she wanted to hurt you, she would have. She went between you and your friend, you said, right?"

"Yes," Carly said. "She flew straight between us."

"Then she was not attacking you. She was warning you, like I said. Warning you about what, I have no idea. You will have to ask you that yourself."

"I didn't think ghosts could hurt people."

"Oh, they can. They can scratch you, pull your hair. If they build up enough energy, they have the ability to move things as well."

"Is Trinny here with me now?" Carly asked.

Madam Hornbeck looked around the room, then back at Carly. "No, she is not here with you today."

"I've done a lot of reading up on ghosts, but I still have a lot of questions."

"Like what?" Madam Hornbeck asked.

"Why doesn't she just cross over to the other side. Why is she still here?" Carly asked.

"Most of the time when spirits remain it is because they have unfinished business or they were killed so quickly and violently that they don't realize they are dead."

"Which is the reason for Trinny?"

"I don't know," Madam Hornbeck said. "Maybe both."

Carly shuddered to think that Trinny may have died a horrible, violent death. She didn't like the idea that she might have unfinished business either. What could it be? What had she not accomplished in life, that she was trying to accomplish now?

"I really appreciate you taking the time to talk to me again today, Madam Hornbeck," Carly said. "I don't know what I would do without your help. There are some who told me to stay away from you. That you're a cracked pot or a nut job. I don't believe that."

"Thank you, my dear," Madam Hornbeck said, unfazed by Carly's comment about what others thought of her. "There are a lot of people out there who are afraid to believe. And when people are afraid, they ridicule. I'm not offended by it. I don't waste any energy on letting it worry me what other people think. I have more important things to spend my energy on."

"So what do I do now?" Carly asked.

"Go home and relax," Madam Hornbeck said. "When you see her again, let her come through. Let her make the first move. Listen. Talk back to her. There is no need to be afraid."

They walked back out to the front room and Carly remembered the crystals. "Is there a crystal that can help me?"

Madam Hornbeck smiled patiently at her. "You are more than welcome to take a crystal if you think it will help, but I don't believe you need one. You're already communicating with a spirit. You just need to learn how to do it without being afraid."

Carly thanked Madam Hornbeck again and walked out the door.

Her mind was still in a whirl and her thoughts just kept piling up one on top of the other.

She needed someone to talk to. But who? Joe? No. He didn't believe her and he just kept trying to convince her that she was imagining it all. Rick? No. He would just tell her to go talk to Joe. Who then?

Just then, a sweet, pleasant face drifted across her mind's eye.

Of course!

Carly jumped in her car and headed to the library.

Chapter 17

Making a quick stop at the pastry shop, Carly grabbed half a dozen assorted donuts, two coffees and headed across the street to the library to go see Sue Langston.

Stepping into the building, Carly was relieved to see only one older gentleman at one of the computers. The rest of the library was empty, except for Sue, who was standing behind the welcome desk.

"Carly," Sue said to her cheerfully. "It's so nice to see you again. Are those for me?" She was looking at the pastry box Carly had tucked under her arm and the coffee cups she was carrying.

Carly laughed and set the items down on a table near the desk. "Yes, they are."

"Oh, I do love donuts...and coffee," said Sue, pulling up a seat at the table. "So, what brings you in here today?"

"I just really needed a friend to talk to," Carly said. "It's been a rough couple of days."

"Well, pull up a chair and tell me all about it," Sue said.

Carly slid into the chair across from Sue and began to spill her guts to the woman.

Sue listened intently and offered the customary "*uh-huh*" and "*oh my*" whenever the situation called for it.

"So what do you think?" Carly asked, when she had finished telling her everything.

"Sounds like you've had a rough couple of days, for sure," Sue said. "I'm glad you went to see Madam Hornbeck. I know a lot of folks around here think she's one brick short of a load, but I tell you, she's the real deal."

"She's helped me a lot," Carly said. "I just need to learn how to communicate with Trinny. Is there anything you can tell me about her?"

Sue pondered the question for a moment. She sipped her coffee, then setting the cup down on the table, she reached for a donut. "Trinny was a really sweet girl. Everyone who knew her, liked her." She took a bite of the donut, chewing it up before speaking again. "But, just like your aunt, she didn't come around much."

"What did she do when she came to town? Who were her friends?" Carly asked.

"Oh, the usual, I suppose. She would go to the grocery store, the bank, maybe stop in over at the beauty shop. She came in here about once a month or so. As for friends, I don't know of any in particular. Again, just like your aunt, it was rumored that she was seeing someone, but she never spoke to me about it, so I don't know who it could have been."

"No idea?" Carly asked.

"No, not really," Sue said. "All I know is that whenever she came in here, she was always very nice and pleasant. I always looked forward to seeing her."

Carly was about to ask more questions when the door to the library opened and Rick walked in.

Rick immediately noticed Carly sitting there with his mother and strolled over to them. He was carrying a box of pastries and two coffees. Carly almost laughed at the thought that he was bringing donuts and coffee to his mother as well, but thought better of it. The last conversation she had with Rick hadn't gone well and she didn't want to start this one off by laughing at him.

"Carly," he said, as he nodded to her. "Mom." He leaned down and gave his mother a peck on the cheek. "Mind if I join you?"

"Why, Rick," Sue said. "Of course not. Why would we mind? Carly was just telling me about the rough week she's had, poor thing."

Rick glanced at Carly, then pulled up a chair next to his mother. "Oh, she has, has she," he said. Carly wasn't able to determine from the sound of his voice whether he was being facetious or whether his flat tone indicated boredom.

Grabbing up a donut and cramming a huge bite into his mouth, he looked directly at Carly and asked, "Can I talk to you for a minute, please?"

"I...uh...sure," Carly stammered, looking sheepishly at Sue. "We'll only be a moment."

Standing up again, he pulled Carly's seat out for her and took her gently by the arm and led her just out of earshot of his mother. "Listen," he said. "I just want to apologize for my behavior before. I acted like a real donkey's rear end. I was just jealous. I thought you and me had really hit it off and then, when I saw you with Joe, I realized I had made a mistake, that you were actually in a relationship with him. I got mad. I'm really sorry."

Carly felt a huge weight lift off her shoulders. "Of course, I forgive you," she said. "I guess I should have told you about Joe and me, but I figured you already knew since he was at the house with me that first time I called the cops. I just assumed you knew. I'm sorry, too."

"Still friends?" Rick asked, holding out his hand for a truce handshake.

"Of course, "Carly said, shaking his hand.

"I'm assuming you didn't tell my mom about our fight?"

"No, I didn't."

"Good, then we don't need to tell her," Rick said, laughing. "She'll just read more into it than there really is."

Carly agreed and they returned to the table.

After they munched on donuts and finished off their coffees, the conversation turned back to Carly's troubles.

"So," Sue asked. "Have you had a chance to hunt for Ruth's *hidden treasure*?"

"I still don't know what that's supposed to mean," Carly said. "What could she have had that would be worth more than that property and her fortune?"

"Oh, who knows," Sue said, sounding bored with the topic. "No one has ever been able to figure that aunt of yours out."

"Maybe she's got something hidden around the place that no one knows about," Rick offered, shrugging his shoulders. "If there is something there, you'll eventually find it, I'm sure."

"I wouldn't even know what to look for," Carly said.

"Rick," Sue said, changing the subject. "Carly was asking about Trinny. Do you know anything about her that you could share with her? I just don't know that much."

Rick thought for a second, then said, "She was a really nice woman. I didn't know her very well, but what few times I ran into her, she was very nice, very sweet."

"Do you know of any friends that she had, or who she was seeing?"

Rick looked at her shocked. "You mean Joe didn't tell you?"

"Tell me what?" A cold feeling washed over Carly. She already knew what Rick was going to say before he said it, but she didn't want to hear it.

"She was seeing Joe there for awhile," Rick said. "They were dating."

Carly felt the bottom drop out of her stomach. "What?" she asked, barely able to breathe. Why wouldn't Joe have told her this. This was important. He had dated her sister and couldn't be bothered to tell her?

"Carly, I'm sorry," Rick said, looking very uncomfortable. "I thought you knew. Joe should have told you."

Carly pushed her chair back and stood up. She couldn't think. Her head was spinning and she couldn't seem to focus.

Grabbing her purse, she turned to leave.

"Let me walk you out," Rick offered. "You don't look so good."

Sue quickly got to her feet and came around to Carly. "Are you alright, dear?"

Carly nodded, but stared blankly at the floor. "Yes, I'm fine. I just need to go home."

"Rick, make sure she gets there safely, will you?" Sue asked Rick.

"Of course," Rick said. He took Carly by the arm and led her to the door.

They stepped outside, but instead of walking to her car, he led her around the corner to his truck.

"Where are we going?" Carly asked him. "I'm parked across the street."

"I know," Rick said. "But I'm going to take you home. You're in no shape to drive."

"No, I'm fine," Carly said. "It was just a shock to learn that Joe dated Trinny and never bothered to tell me. I'm fine. Really."

Rick gently pulled Carly into his arms and hugged her. It was a comforting hug, a friendly hug. "I'm sorry you had to find out like this."

Carly leaned into his embrace and let out a long sigh. "Seems I'm finding out all sorts of things. My house is haunted. I have, or rather had, a half sister, whose trying to communicate with me. Now I find out Joe was dating her. It's all just a lot to take in."

"You've been through a lot," Rick said. "It's going to be ok, though. You're not alone. You have me...and mom."

Carly looked up at him. His green eyes seemed to be piercing through her. Her heartbeat quickened as her eyes grazed over his face and down to his lips.

Seeming to understand her unspoken thoughts, Rick leaned down and pressed his lips against hers. She started to pull back, but decided to just give in to the temptation. She opened her mouth and pressed her lips hard against his.

The kiss left her reeling. Instantly, guilt washed over her. She stepped back from him and wiped her hand across her mouth. "Rick," she said, breathlessly. "I'm so sorry. I don't know what I was thinking. I was just upset and...."

Rick reached out and put his hands on her shoulders. "I'm sorry, too," he said. "I took advantage of the situation. It won't happen again."

"It was my fault," Carly said. "I have to go."

Carly turned and walked back to her car feeling horrible. What had she just done? She was mad at Joe for not telling her that he had dated Trinny. Meanwhile, she's locking lips with the hot police officer.

She crawled behind the wheel of her car and slammed the door shut. "Stupid, stupid, stupid," she said, smacking her forehead with the palm of her hand.

She drove home feeling numb inside. Did she feel something for Rick? What about Joe? She really liked Joe. He was fun to be around, but she had to admit, they seemed to butt heads a lot. Especially about the whole Trinny thing. But, then again, Rick didn't believe her either. She was very confused and didn't know what to think.

Suddenly, Madam Hornbeck's words came back to her. She had told her to trust her heart and not to fight it. The problem was, she didn't know which man her heart wanted.

Lost in her thoughts, she whipped into her driveway and slammed on the brakes when she reached the house.

Still angry with herself for kissing Rick, she slammed the car door shut and started to climb the steps to the front door, when a sound reached her that sent chills up spine.

"Cccaaarrrlllyyy…," a voice called to her. It was faint, but she definitely heard it.

She stopped moving and listened again.

"Ccaarrllyy…," it came again, even fainter than before.

It was coming from around the side of the house. Who was calling her name? It wasn't Trinny's voice this time. In fact, it sounded like Vernon's.

Dropping her purse, she rushed down the steps and along the stone path that wrapped around the side of the house. She rounded the corner and found Vernon slumped over, sitting on the ground outside of the carriage house.

Rushing over to him, she dropped down on her knees and leaned over him. "Vernon! What happened?" she asked him.

He was holding his left arm and blood was dripping down between his fingers.

"I was trimming the bushes and fell," he said, his breathing was labored. "I cut my arm. I think it's broken."

Carly noticed the pool of blood on the ground beside him and the dark stains that covered his shirt and pants.

"Oh Vernon," Carly said. "How long have you been sitting here waiting for me to come home?"

"About an hour, I suppose."

Vernon was pale and obviously in a lot of pain. Carly's problems flew out of her head as she was now worried about him.

"Stay here," she told him. "I'm going to go get a towel and call an ambulance." She jumped to her feet and prepared to run to the house, but Vernon stopped her.

"No, Carly," he said. "It'll take too long for them to get here. You'll have to take me."

Carly bolted for the house. She quickly unlocked the front door and ran for the bathroom, grabbing a couple of towels. She thought about grabbing some peroxide, too, but knew the hospital would do a better job of cleaning it up than she would, so she raced back outside with just the towels.

Quickly wrapping one of the towels around his injured arm, she grabbed him under his other arm and tried to lift him up, but even though he was old and rather thin, she was a tiny woman herself and lifting him was proving impossible.

"You're going to have to help me, Vernon," she said, still straining to lift him up. "I can't do it by myself."

Vernon used what little bit of strength he had left, and hoisted himself up onto his feet. Carly quickly threw his arm around her shoulders and helped him around the side of the house to the car.

After getting him situated in the car and making him as comfortable as she could, she fastened his seat belt for him and tucked the towel securely under his arm.

She quickly ran around to the other side of the car and scrambled into the driver's seat. Starting the car, she took off down the driveway and drove as quickly as she could to the hospital.

She pulled up to the emergency room doors and got out, leaving Vernon sitting in the car. She raced inside, looking for someone to help her. She knew there was no way she could lift him out of the car and walk him all the way inside by herself. Getting him to the car at the house had taken a lot out of her. His dead weight had made it difficult to get him around the house and into the car and she knew it had wasted precious time. She was in a panic. He had lost so much blood and kept trying to go to sleep on her the whole way to the hospital.

She found a nurse walking down a hallway and ran up to her, quickly explaining to her what was going on. The nurse grabbed a wheelchair and followed her out to the car.

When they opened the car door, Vernon was slumped forward in the seat. Carly sucked in a breath, not realizing that tears were running down her cheeks. Had he died while she was inside looking for someone to help? She just stood there staring at his slumped body for a moment when the nurse touched her arm.

"I'm going to need you to step aside, ma'am, so I can get him out of there," the nurse said to her.

Carly quickly stepped back and watched as the nurse took over and got Vernon into the wheelchair. Rushing him inside, she told Carly to go park the car and meet them in the waiting room.

Carly parked the car in the nearest spot she could find, which was clear across the parking lot from the entrance. She ran as fast as she could into the emergency room waiting area, frantically looking around for Vernon.

The nurse who had assisted her with Vernon came up to her and escorted her back to the room they had put him in to wait on the doctor.

Throwing the curtain back, Carly looked at Vernon laying helplessly in the bed. He was so pale and pasty looking. His white hair was all askew and his mouth was hanging open. His eyes were shut and for a moment, she thought he was dead.

His dirty, stained clothes were laying in a pile on the chair beside the bed and he was wrapped in an ugly, green hospital gown.

Walking softly to the side of the bed, she gently reached for his hand and held it between both of hers.

"Vernon?" she asked softly. "Are you awake?"

Vernon opened his eyes and blinked up at her. "Carly," he said. "It's going to be ok. I lost a lot of blood, but I've been through worse. You aren't going to get rid of me that easily."

Carly couldn't help but chuckle. Still the same old, grumpy man he always was.

"You really scared me, you know," she scolded him.

"I scared myself, too."

The curtain was pushed aside and a young doctor with a clipboard in his hand came into the tiny cubicle, followed by the nurse. "Hello," he said. "I'm Doctor Sims."

Carly watched as the doctor examined Vernon's arm and gave instructions to the nurse for x-rays, and lab work. Turning to Carly, he asked. "Are you his daughter?"

"No," she told him. "He's my...friend."

"I'm sorry," he said. "You'll have to wait in the waiting room. No one other than family is allowed back here."

Carly glanced down at Vernon, then back to the doctor. "But, I'm all he has."

"If you aren't family, you can't be back here, miss. I'm sorry. Hospital rules."

Vernon nodded his head at Carly and she stepped out of the room.

The waiting room was just down the hall from the room Vernon was in. The tv was tuned to some news channel, but the volume was turned off.

Taking a seat next to the window, Carly grabbed up a magazine that was laying on a table and flipped through its pages while she waited for word on Vernon.

Over an hour later, the nurse came into the room and told Carly she could come back and see him now.

Throwing the magazine back onto the table, she quickly jumped to her feet, almost running the nurse over to get back to Vernon's room.

Vernon was sitting up in the bed, a stack of pillows behind his head. A cast was covering his left arm and an I.V. was stuck in the back of his hand.

His color was back and he actually looked happy to see her.

"I was right," he said, indicating his left arm. "It's broken."

Carly leaned over and planted a light kiss on the top of his head. "Silly old man," she said, kindly.

"The doc said I was lucky," Vernon told her. "I had to have five stitches in my arm to close up the wound and now I have to wear this old cast for six weeks till my arm heals up."

"How does that make you lucky?" Carly asked.

"He said if you hadn't found me when you did, I probably would have bled to death."

"Oh Vernon," Carly said. "That cut must have been really bad. I'm so sorry I wasn't home when you got hurt."

"It wasn't your fault, missy. You're not my babysitter."

"I know, but I feel so bad."

"Well, stop it. It don't do no good to feel that way. I'm fine. Just needed a little fixing up is all. Doc said I'm going to be staying overnight here so they can keep an eye on me, though."

"That's understandable," Carly said.

"Could you do me a favor?" Vernon asked.

"Of course. Anything."

"I need you to bring me some clean clothes in the morning when you come pick me up. I don't really want to wear the ones I came in here with. They're a bit dirty and bloody."

"Sure. I just need the key to your house," Carly said.

Vernon told her to dig the key out of his pants pocket that was laying on the chair.

Fishing around in his pants, she pulled out a key ring that had several keys dangling from it. She grabbed up his clothes and tucked them under her arm just as the nurse came back in.

"Time to get you up to your room, Mr. Knowles," she said, cheerfully. "Miss, we'll probably discharge him around ten or so in the morning. Are you the one who will picking him up?"

"Yes," Carly said.

"Make sure you're here around ten then just to be sure you're here when they discharge him."

Carly nodded at the nurse, then turned to Vernon. "I'll see you in the morning," she said.

Vernon nodded at her and gave her a small smile.

Carly walked out to her car and flopped down into the driver's seat, feeling drained.

She threw Vernon's dirty clothes onto the passenger side and began the drive home.

It had been such a long day and it was only six o'clock.

Feeling worn out and tired, Carly parked the car and began climbing the steps to the front door when she remembered Vernon's clothes that he would need in the morning.

Figuring it was best to get them now, she dropped her purse and the dirty pile of Vernon's clothes on the veranda and walked around to the carriage house.

She fumbled around with the keys trying to find the right one to unlock the door.

Finally a key slid into the lock and she swung the door open.

She wasn't familiar with the layout of his house, so she poked her head into each room until she found his bedroom, which was at the back of the house.

Flipping on the light switch, she looked around the room.

There was a small bed and a nightstand up against the back wall. A single dresser stood next to the door. Heading for the dresser first, she began pulling out a pair of underwear, socks and pants and threw them onto the bed.

Next, she opened up the closet door and flipped through the hangers of clothing until she found a light blue shirt she thought would work.

She was just getting ready to close the door when something caught her eye. A small flash of silver. Curious about the man she barely knew, she wondered what it was.

Standing on her tiptoes, she reached up onto the shelf above the rack of clothes and nudged a box aside that was half hiding the object.

She still couldn't quite see what it was, so she stepped into the closet a little further and shoved the box over a little more and craned her neck to see what was behind it.

It was a silver, lopsided, heart shaped necklace draped over a light rose colored urn trimmed in silver with a heart etched into the front of it. The words, *Ruth Constance Montgomery,* were engraved in silver below the heart.

Carly stared in shock at the necklace and urn.

Slowly, the truth began to dawn on her. The necklace was Aunt Ruth's, which she had already figured. But why would Vernon have it draped over her aunt's urn hidden in the back of his closet? Why did he have her aunt's urn?

Because Vernon loved her Aunt Ruth. He must have given Aunt Ruth that necklace. That's why he had demanded that it wasn't hers and she had no right to wear it. Vernon was Aunt Ruth's secret love!

Gently removing the necklace from the urn, Carly stuffed it into her pocket. She didn't bother moving the box back in front of the urn. The secret was out.

Grabbing the clothes off the bed, she hurried back to the mansion.

Vernon had some explaining to do and this time, she wouldn't take no for an answer!

Chapter 18

By the time Carly got home, she was exhausted. Not so much physically, as mentally. Her mind was still reeling from learning about Joe and Trinny, then finding out that Vernon was Aunt Ruth's lover. It was all so much to take in.

She threw a frozen pizza in the oven, then grabbed up Vernon's dirty, bloody clothes and tossed them into the washer.

She really needed to talk to Joe. She needed him to explain to her why he never told her about Trinny. Her heart was aching and if she gave in to it, she was afraid that she would break down and start crying. She hated crying.

The timer on the oven buzzed. She removed the pizza and set it on the stove. Pouring herself a glass of iced tea, she pulled a bar stool up to the island and began to eat.

Her mind just wouldn't move off the topic of Joe and Trinny, so whipping out her phone, she punched in Joe's number.

"Hey, Carly," came his voice over the phone.

"Joe," Carly said. She knew her voice sounded angry, but she felt justified. "We need to talk."

"Sure. What's up?" The phone crackled as if he was talking while wadding up a piece of paper near the mouth piece.

"Where are you?" Carly asked. "You're breaking up. I'm having a hard time hearing you."

"I have...make...trip...to...building supplies...job....next week," came his broken statement.

"Why didn't you tell me you were leaving? When are you coming back?"

"Last min...should...back....late tomorrow."

"Fine," Carly said, exasperated. "Call me as soon as you get home. Or better yet, come over."

No response.

"Joe?"

The line went dead.

"Great!" Carly groaned, slamming the phone down.

She didn't finish all the pizza, but the couple of slices she did eat she hadn't really enjoyed. It just tasted like cardboard to her. If she hadn't been hungry, she would have just thrown the whole thing in the trash.

Why didn't Joe tell her he was leaving? It would have only taken a moment or two to call her and let her know.

Feeling more annoyed than before, she cleaned up the kitchen and switched the laundry over to the dryer.

She huffed her way into the sitting room and threw herself onto one of the couches that sat near the fireplace.

As she sat there staring into space, her mind a million miles away, her phone rang.

Hoping it was Joe, she yanked it out of her back pocket and saw that it was Rick.

Did she want to answer it? She was still really embarrassed about her forward behavior with him that afternoon. He was just one more thing that had her mind in a tizzle.

Deciding her curiosity was greater than her embarrassment, she tapped the talk button and said, "Hi Rick."

"Hey," Rick said. "I just wanted to call and see how you were doing. You seemed pretty upset this afternoon."

"Truthfully, I'm not much better."

"Did something else happen? Did you talk to Joe?"

Did she note a sound of hopefulness in his voice? She knew he wanted to date her, but would he really hope things went sour with Joe just so he could have a chance? She sure hoped not. Rick was such a sweet guy and she genuinely liked him. She didn't want to think he would be happy about something that hurt her.

"No, I haven't been able to talk to him yet," she said. "He had to run out of town for supplies for an upcoming job he has next week and he won't be back till late tomorrow. I'll just have to wait till he gets home."

"Carly, I'm so sorry," Rick said. "I know how hard this is on you."

"Yeah, it is," Carly said. "It really stinks."

"Do you want to talk about it?"

"What's there to say? Joe lied to me. Or rather, purposely omitted a very important fact that would have been nice to know. Why would he do that? What's he hiding?"

"I don't know, Carly," Rick said. "Don't jump to conclusions, though. Maybe he has a good explanation for it."

"He'd better," Carly said.

"So what are your plans for the evening now that Joe is out of the picture?"

"A long, hot bath, a good book and some peace and quiet, I hope."

"Sounds like a good idea," Rick said.

"Oh," Carly said. "I forgot to tell you about Vernon."

"What about him?"

"He fell today and cut and broke his arm while I was at the library. I came home and found him sitting on the ground outside of his house waiting on me."

"Is he ok?"

Carly could hear the concern in Rick's voice. It made her feel better to think he really cared.

"Yes, he is now. I took him to the emergency room. He had to have stitches and a cast put on, but he'll be fine. They're going to keep him overnight for observation. He lost a lot of blood from the cut."

"That's horrible. I'm glad he's ok, though," Rick said.

"Me too."

"If you're sure you're ok, then I'll let you get to your bath and book," Rick said. "I just wanted to check on you."

"Thanks, Rick," Carly said. "I really appreciate it."

"If you need anything, just call, ok?"

"I will," Carly promised. "Good night."

"Good night, Carly."

Carly sat on the couch for a few more minutes pondering her feelings toward Rick. He was always so thoughtful and kind. A part of her wished he was here. The other part of her wished Joe was. It was hard being attracted to two men at the same time. She really couldn't decide which one she liked better.

She got up off the couch and decided to head upstairs and start her bath.

As she passed the mirror in the hallway, she stopped and gazed into the glass for a long moment. Where was Trinny tonight? She hadn't seen nor heard from her since the cemetery.

Looking into the mirror, she half hoped to see her step up behind her and half hoped not to. If she did, would she run away or finally be able to face her and talk to her?

As she stared into the mirror, she wasn't sure what her reaction would be. She didn't want to be afraid, but she had to admit, after the incident in the cemetery, she wasn't so sure she wouldn't be. Madam Hornbeck had told her not to be afraid, but Madam Hornbeck hadn't seen Trinny the way Carly had... angry and shrieking.

Carly dragged her feet as she climbed the stairs. She was not in a good mood and was hoping the hot bath would help her relax and ease her mind a bit.

She turned down the hall and headed toward her room.

She turned on the taps to let the tub fill up with water as she stripped off her clothing.

Remembering the necklace in her pocket, she pulled it out and looked at it.

It really was a simple, but beautiful, necklace.

Not wanting to lose it, she took it to her room and stuffed it down into a pocket inside her purse.

At least one mystery was solved, she thought. She knew who had broken into her house that first time and who had stolen the necklace. It was Vernon. Why hadn't he just asked her for it? Because he didn't want her to know about him and her aunt. But why? Was he the one who had broken in all the other times as well, and if so, what was he looking for? She was anxious to talk to him about it, but that would have to wait till tomorrow.

She eased herself down into the hot, steamy water and laid her head back on the rim of the tub and let the anger, stress and fear of the last couple of days leave her body. She closed her eyes and took several deep breaths and slowly released them.

She must have dozed off for a moment. She came awake when she heard a soft whisper calling her name.

"Ccaarrllyy..."

Siting up in the tub, Carly looked around the room, but didn't see anything.

The room was steamy which made seeing anything difficult, but she knew Trinny was there.

Gripping the sides of the tub, Carly sat up straight and looked around the room again. "Trinny? I know you're here."

"Carly," Trinny's voice was clear and close by.

Carly was shaking with nerves, but was determined to face her sister without running away. "Trinny, where are you? I can't see you."

Slowly, the mist began to gather in the center of the room. Little by little it took on the shape of a woman.

As Carly watched, a beautiful woman, so much like herself, stood before her. She was translucent and her form was wispy, but she was there.

"Hi," Carly said shakily. "It's nice to finally meet you." She gulped a couple of times trying to squelch down the fear that was rising in her.

Trinny floated across the floor until she was standing beside the tub looking down at Carly. "Carly," she said. "Don't trust him."

"Don't trust who?"

"He's evil, Carly," Trinny's voice was so soft and lightly spoken that Carly had to strain to hear her.

"Who, Trinny? Whose evil?"

"Watch out, things aren't what they seem."

Trinny's form was beginning to fade. Carly reached out to grab her to keep her from leaving, but her hand slipped through the misty form and wrapped around nothing but air. "Trinny, who? Who are you warning me about?"

Trinny had disappeared, but her disembodied voice floated to Carly through the steam. "He's watching you. Be careful." With that, Trinny was gone.

Carly jumped out of the tub and quickly dried herself off. She threw on a pair of jeans and a shirt and dashed out of the room.

She began searching the house one room at a time. Who was watching her? Who was Trinny warning her about? Joe? Rick? Vernon? Or someone else?

Carly checked out every room in the house, but she was the only one there.

Breathing out a frustrated sigh of relief, she made her way back to her bedroom.

"Trinny, if you're here, please come talk to me. I searched the house, but no one is here. What did you mean? Whose watching me?" Her question was met with nothing but total silence.

Throwing her clothes into a pile on the floor, she slipped her nightgown on and crawled into bed.

An uneasy feeling came over her. Was someone really watching her? And if so, why? Who was Trinny trying to tell her was evil? Everyone she met so far was very kind. She couldn't imagine any of them doing anything to hurt her.

Suddenly, her mind when back to something Joe had said to her the day she had bumped her head and he took her to the urgent care clinic. He had told her, "I never want to hurt you." A chill ran up Carly's spine. At the time she had wondered what he had meant by it, but she had just blown it off. Now she was wondering if maybe it had been a warning. Maybe he was warning her that he cared about her, but he was capable of hurting her. But, if that was so, what could possibly make him want to her hurt?

She tried to relax, but her mind wouldn't let her. She kept replaying all the events that had happened since she moved here. Nothing was making sense.

Too many questions kept popping into her head, but she didn't have answers for any of them.

Finally, exhaustion took over and she drifted into a fitful sleep.

Chapter 19

Carly tossed and turned. In her dreams, she was running through a foggy cemetery being chased by an angry Trinny. She kept running in circles around the headstone of Rutherford Montgomery, but was never able to run away from it.

Suddenly, a noise jolted her out of her dreams.

Ssscccrrraaapppeee.....

Carly's eyes flew open and she sat bolt upright in bed. Listening intently, she waited to see if she would hear the noise again.

Ssccaappee.....

She froze. She was familiar with that sound by now. But where was it coming from? What was making the noise? She sat on the bed for several long moments, but no more scraping sounds reached her ears.

Tossing the covers aside, she threw her legs over the side of the bed and started to get up.

"Cccaaarrrlllyyy..."

Carly stopped and looked around the darkened room. "Trinny?"

Trinny's ghostly form began to appear at the foot of her bed. Her long, dark hair was almost covering her face and her sickly, white arm was raised in the air toward Carly. The white gown she wore was tattered and torn and even in ghostly form, it was dirty and stained. "Ccaarrllyy, come," she beckoned her.

Carly stared at Trinny. Her image was sharper and clearer than it had been before and even her voice was stronger.

She wasn't sure if she trusted following her, though, as flashbacks of the cemetery flashed across her mind.

"Are you going to get angry with me again? You really scared me in the cemetery. Why were you so angry at me?" Carly asked her.

"Wouldn't pay attention. Needed you to know. Don't want to hurt you. Need help," Trinny said, her voice sounding hollow, but firm.

"Needed me to know what?"

"Come," was all Trinny said, pointing her arm toward the door.

"Where are you taking me?" Carly asked, slipping off the bed and walking cautiously toward her.

"Come," Trinny said again, as her ghostly image turned and glided out the door of the bedroom and into the hall.

Carly hesitated. She had just heard the odd scraping sound again and didn't relish the idea of roaming around the house not knowing what or where the sounds might have come from.

"Come," Trinny called to her again, when she hesitated at the door.

Carly turned and grabbed her cell phone off the night table and quietly slipped out the door and tiptoed down the hall after Trinny.

It was dark in the house. No lights were on and no moonlight was shining down from any of the windows. The only light seemed to be coming from Trinny's white, glowing, ethereal body.

Trinny glided down the hall and stopped at the top of the stairs waiting for Carly to catch up.

When Carly was almost to her, Trinny turned and floated down the steps silently.

Carly watched Trinny float down over each step, though she never actually touched one of them.

When she reached the bottom, Trinny turned right, then disappeared into the sitting room.

Carly stepped down off the last step and turned the corner into the sitting room behind Trinny.

She watched as Trinny drifted across the room and walked straight into the fireplace and vanished.

Carly rushed over and waited to see if Trinny would reappear out of the fireplace, but she didn't. She had simply walked into it and disappeared. "Trinny?" she called to her in a whisper. "Trinny, where are you?"

Carly pressed her hand against the mantle and leaned down and looked into the fireplace, but no Trinny.

Leaning down farther, she craned her neck and looked up the chimney, but still no ghostly glow was seen.

Dropping down onto her knees, she crawled forward and stuck her head inside the fireplace, but could not see anything in the pitch blackness of the small alcove.

As she stood up, she felt something gritty on her fingers. She brushed her hands across the front of her nightgown and stood up.

If she was going to be able to see in there, she would need a flashlight.

Carly assumed it was the wee hours of the morning since it was so dark, but had never actually checked the time.

Lifting her phone close to her face, she squeezed the power button that illuminated the face of the phone.

3:45 a.m.

She pulled up the flashlight app on the phone, then turned it toward the fireplace. She surveyed the small cavity, but couldn't see anything out of place or anywhere that Trinny could have gone.

She turned the phone toward her hands and saw a thick, black, gritty substance smeared across her fingers.

Soot.

Just like the soot that was on her attic door a couple of nights ago.

Just as she was getting to her feet, she heard a muffled thud come from overhead.

Looking up at the ceiling, she realized it was coming from somewhere upstairs.

She clicked the light off on her phone and looked around one more time for Trinny.

Not seeing her anywhere, Carly tiptoed out into the hallway to the foot of the stairs.

Thump...

The sound definitely came from upstairs.

Taking one step at a time, Carly slowly climbed the stairs.

With each step, she would pause and listen. When no noise was heard, she would take another step.

When she finally reached the top of the stairs, she stood in the dark and listened.

A muffled scrape and a soft thump could be heard overhead.

The attic.

Someone was in her house again. In the attic. What were they looking for? It couldn't be Vernon this time. He was still in the hospital.

Carly scampered back to her room looking for a weapon. If she was going to face this intruder, she would need something to protect herself with.

Looking around frantically for anything that could be used, she realized the only place that might have something was the kitchen.

A knife. She could get a knife from the kitchen.

Holding her breath, she tiptoed to the bedroom door and glanced down the hallway to the far end where the attic door was.

It was too dark to see if anyone stood there looking back at her, but she didn't think the attic door was open. She couldn't make out the ladder leaning down toward the floor in the shadowy darkness.

She quickly made her way to the top of the stairs and down the steps to the kitchen.

She felt her way along the wall with her hands all the way to the island and around to the counter on the other side.

Feeling along the counter, she found the knife block, and fumbling around, finally wrapped her fingers around the handle of a large carving knife.

Pulling it slowly from its nesting place so it wouldn't make a noise, she gripped the handle tight in her hand and turned to leave the kitchen.

From somewhere overhead she heard what sounded like footsteps walking across the floor.

Holding the knife out in front of her as she walked, she quietly made her way back down the hall and up the stairs to the second floor.

Once she reached the landing, she turned left and tiptoed as quietly as she could to the end of the hall.

A small swath of moonlight filtered in through the large window, allowing just enough light for her to see the string hanging down from the attic door.

Reaching up, she gently tugged the string until the door popped open and swung down.

She craned her head toward the opening, listening to see if she heard any noises coming from the space above, but only silence greeted her.

She pulled the ladder down and looked up into the dark cavity of the attic above.

Did she really want to crawl up there if someone was already up there waiting for her? Not really, but what choice did she have? She wanted to know who was coming into the house. And how were they getting in without tripping the alarm? What were they looking for? She was tired of all the unanswered questions. So, with her mind made up, she slowly ascended the ladder, one rung at a time.

Reaching the top, she flipped on the overhead lights. The single row of low voltage bulbs flickered to life, illuminating the center aisle of the large room.

Quickly jerking her head around in all directions, she didn't see or hear anything that would have alerted her to someone else's presence.

Climbing the rest of the way into the attic, she scanned both sides of the center aisle as she made her way to the back where the chest she had drug out earlier in the week was still sitting in the middle of the room.

She leaned down and examined the trunk, but it appeared to be just as she'd left it.

Turning around, she slowly headed back the way she had come, the knife held out in front of her.

As she passed a tall stack of boxes next to an old, dilapidated dresser, a movement caught her eye.

Glancing back into the darkness, she thought she saw a figure step back deeper into the shadows.

"I see you back there," she warned. "Who are you? What do you want?"

No one responded. Holding the knife tightly in her hand, she stepped off the center aisle and took several steps back toward the spot where she had seen the figure.

Squinting her eyes to see better, she maneuvered her way past stacks of boxes and piled up junk.

Just as she got to the dresser, a stack of boxes suddenly came tumbling down on top of her.

The corner of a box hit her in the wrist causing her to drop the knife, which skittered across the floor and out of reach.

She raised her hands to deflect the boxes, but there were too many of them and the contents made them heavy. She crumpled to the floor under their weight.

Just as she hit the floor, she saw a person wearing a black ski mask walk up behind the dresser and shove it over...right on top of her.

The corner of the dresser gouged into one of the boxes that had landed on top of her, preventing the dresser from falling directly on top of her.

The weight of the boxes and the dresser kept her pinned to the floor.

As she struggled under the weight, she could hear the masked intruder run across the floor and down the aisle toward the door opening and heard the *thump thump thump* of their foot falls on the ladder rungs as they descended down them. The clunk of the door slamming shut let her know she was now all alone.

The intruder had flipped the light switch off on their way out of the attic leaving Carly in total darkness.

Struggling again to remove the boxes from on top of her, she realized it was useless. They were just too heavy. Plus the weight of the old dresser was pressing down on the box that was sitting on her chest. Each time she struggled, the box seemed to press down even harder.

Panic began to well up in her. She couldn't move and each time she tried, the box and dresser crushed down on her making it hard to breathe. She was running out of air in her lungs and every time she exhaled, it was harder and harder to suck in more air.

Tears filled her eyes and slowly rolled down her cheeks. She was going to die here. Alone in the attic.

Suddenly she felt something in her left hand. Something cold and metallic.

Her phone.

She still had a hold of her phone.

Lifting her hand, she squeezed the phone hoping to press the button that would illuminate the face of the phone. It lit up and using her thumb, swiped the screen till it opened the phone for use.

Gingerly, so she wouldn't drop the phone, she used her thumb to hit the call button. Then scrolling down through her contacts, she came to Joe's number and touched it with the pad of her thumb.

She could hear it ringing and ringing, but Joe never picked up. She heard his recorded message telling her to leave her name and number and he would call back.

Tears running down her cheeks in earnest now, she tapped the end button and went back to her contacts.

Flipping through the names listed in alphabetical order, she found Rick's.

Tapping the call button, she heard it ring.

Once.

Twice.

Three times.

Then… "Hello?"

"Rick," Carly said. She could hardy breath. Each breath was a strain to drag into her lungs. "Help...me."

"Carly?" Rick asked. "What's wrong? Where are you?"

"Attic...boxes fell...trapped." Carly couldn't say anymore. She was getting dizzy and with each word she spoke, her lungs were beginning to burn.

Stars drifted across her vision and her arm felt weak. She dropped the phone, but not before hearing Rick call out. "I'm coming, Carly!"

Carly lay in the dark for what felt like hours. Her lungs burned and the weight of the boxes was beginning to jab into different parts of her body causing sharp, throbbing pain.

She closed her eyes and waited for Rick.

Where was Joe? Why hadn't he answered his phone? Was he still out of cell range?

Where was Trinny? Not that a ghost could help her, but she would have felt better to have some company, even if it was a ghost, then to lay here and die all alone.

Hot tears ran down her cheeks and she let out a sob. The effort sent a stab of pain shooting across her chest. She was about ready to just give in, when she heard the attic door swing open.

Footsteps pounded up the ladder. The lights flickered on and a voice called out to her. "Carly?"

Carly couldn't muster up enough air to call out to him, but a renewed energy filled her at the thought of being rescued, so she kicked one of her feet and hit a box, causing it to slide across the floor.

Rick rushed over to where the sound came from and found Carly's leg sticking out among a pile of boxes.

"Carly, are you alright?" he asked, a sound of panic in his voice. "Can you hear me?"

Carly squeaked out a response and Rick grabbed the corner of the dresser and shoved it off of her with one mighty push. It crashed to the floor behind her head.

He quickly got to work removing all the boxes that had piled up on top of her.

She lay there on the floor, gulping in lungfuls of air. The burning in her chest began to subside and she could finally breathe again.

Rick knelt down beside her and lifted her into a sitting position. He checked her over quickly, assessing her for any injuries. Not finding anything more than a couple of bumps and bruises, he sat down on the floor next to her and asked, "What happened? What are you doing up here in the middle of the night?" Carly noticed the genuine concern in his eyes and suddenly the tears began to fall again.

"I heard a noise and got up to check it out," Carly said, sniffling.

"Hey, it's ok now," Rick said, wrapping his arm around her shoulders and pulling her into his chest.

"Trinny came to my room and got me," Carly told him.

"Trinny came and got you? I don't understand."

"I heard the noise downstairs and Trinny appeared at the foot of my bed and told me to follow her. I did. She took me to the sitting room and then she just walked into the fireplace and disappeared."

"She...walked into the fireplace...and disappeared?" Rick asked, sounding doubtful.

"Yes. I don't know what she was trying to show me, though. As I was waiting for her to return, I heard a thump come from upstairs, so I came up to see who was here."

"Carly, why didn't you call me? I'm a cop. I would have come out and checked it out for you."

"Because I was afraid that, just like before, they would be gone by the time you got here. I want to know who keeps breaking into my house and why, so I came up to see who it was."

"Without a weapon? Carly, they could have killed you."

"I had a weapon. A carving knife. But when the boxes were pushed over on me, I lost it."

"Go on," Rick said. "How did you end up under all the boxes?"

"I was walking down the center aisle when I heard a noise coming from behind the boxes. I called out, but no one answered. I thought I saw someone back here, so I started to walk back and the person pushed the stack of boxes over on me. Then when I fell, I saw the person. They were wearing a black ski mask. That's when they shoved the dresser over on top of me."

"Carly, you could have been killed."

"I know," Carly said. "I did a really stupid thing."

"If you didn't want to call me, you should have called Joe," Rick scolded her.

"I tried," Carly said. "He never answered.

"Hhmmm," Rick said.

"What?"

"Doesn't it seem a bit strange to you that he's conveniently out of town right now? He didn't even bother to tell you he was leaving.

Then when you try to call him after being attacked by someone in your attic, he doesn't answer his phone?"

"What are you saying? That Joe's the one who has been breaking in? That he would have tried to hurt me?"

"Well, it does seem suspicious, that's all."

Carly couldn't deny it looked suspicious. The same thoughts had already crossed her mind. Trinny had warned her not to trust someone. That someone might want to hurt her.

A sudden shiver ran up Carly's spine. No way. She didn't want to believe that Joe would do something like this. He cared about her. He wouldn't want to hurt her, would he?

Getting to her feet, she leaned on Rick as they made their way to the ladder. He smelled good. Too good. And he showed up to help her. He was the one who rescued her.

Looking up into his face, she felt a warmth spread through her. Rick was one of the sweetest men she had ever met. He was genuine. Loved his mother. Helped her out whenever she needed it. He was always there for her. Rick was beginning to win the battle over her heart.

They made it to the kitchen and Carly replaced the knife back into its wooden block. Rick had found it several feet from where Carly had fallen and grabbed it on the way out of the attic.

"I have a question for you, Carly," Rick said. "If someone was roaming around inside your house, why didn't you turn any lights on? Wouldn't that have scared away any intruder?"

"I didn't want the person to know I was aware of them being here. I thought if I left the lights off, I could sneak up on them."

"But you turned the attic lights on," Rick said.

"I was sure they were up there. I thought if I turned the lights on, they would be trapped and I could see who it was. Dumb mistake. They stayed hidden in the shadows and attacked me from behind the boxes where I couldn't see them."

"What about the alarm?" Rick asked. "Didn't it go off?"

"No," Carly said. "There must be something wrong with it."

"I'll check it out again tomorrow."

"Thanks, Rick."

Rick pulled her into his arms and hugged her tight. "I'm just glad you weren't hurt and that I got to you in time."

"Me too," Carly said, leaning in to him.

It felt right being in his arms. She hugged him tighter and a sense of safety filled her.

"It's almost six in the morning," he said to her. "I'd better let you get to bed and try to get a few more hours of sleep. You've had quite a scare and it's time for you to rest a bit."

"Would you mind staying?" Carly asked. "I'm still a bit shaken up and don't really want to be alone."

"Sure," Rick said. "Go grab a blanket and I'll meet you in the sitting room."

Carly looked up at him, shocked. "The sitting room? I thought you'd want to take one of the spare bedrooms?"

"No, if I'm gonna stay, I'm not letting you out of my sight. We can cuddle on the couch and get some sleep there."

Carly stood on her toes so she could reach his lips and pressed her mouth to his. It was a soft, easy kiss, but it made Carly weak in the knees.

Feeling a bit giddy inside, she turned and raced up the stairs to her room.

Once again, she realized she had been caught in nothing but her nightgown. She seemed to be making a habit out of that.

Grabbing her robe and a blanket, she headed back downstairs.

Chapter 20

Carly woke several hours later wrapped up in a blanket on one end of the couch in the sitting room, while Rick was curled up on the other end still sound asleep. Carly gazed at him for a moment before getting up. It warmed her heart that he insisted on staying close to her last night to protect her in case the intruder came back. She felt safe around him. She knew in her heart that she was beginning to fall in love with him.

Quietly throwing the blanket off, she tiptoed to the kitchen to start a pot of coffee.

It wasn't long before Rick joined her. She chuckled when he walked into the kitchen. His hair was all tasseled and he looked dopey.

"Well, good morning, Sunshine," she said as she slid a cup of coffee across the island to him.

Pulling up a seat, he lifted the hot brew to his lips and took a sip. "Good morning to you, too."

"You look like death warmed over," Carly said.

"Yeah, well," Rick said. "That couch wasn't the most comfortable thing I've ever slept on."

"I offered you a guestroom," Carly said, chuckling. "I'm sure the beds are much better than that old couch."

"I'm sure they are," grumbled Rick, though he was grinning.

"Are you on duty today?" Carly asked.

"No, I'm off today. Thought I'd take Mom out to lunch. Want to join us?'

"Oh, I wish I could, but I have to go to the hospital and pick Vernon up and bring him home. Rain check?"

"Sure," Rick said. "Tell Vernon I hope he gets better soon. That little injury is going to put him down for a few weeks."

"Unfortunately," Carly said. "I may have to hire someone to fill in for him while he heals. This place needs constant care and upkeep."

"That's probably a good idea."

"I'd better go get dressed or I'll be late to the hospital," Carly said, downing the last of the coffee in her cup and setting the mug in the sink.

"Do you want me to check the security system before I go?" Rick asked.

"Oh, yes, please. I almost forgot."

"Have you given the access code to anyone?"

"Just Joe," Carly said. "He needed it the other day when he was testing it."

"Wait," Rick said. "You gave the code to Joe?"

"Yes," Carly said. "Why?"

"Carly, I'm not trying to cause trouble here, but he is conveniently out of town right now. You aren't able to get a hold of him. And he has the code for the alarm system. Doesn't that all seem kind of suspicious to you?"

Carly drew her eyebrows together as she thought about what Rick had just said. "Yes, actually, it does."

"I'm not saying it was him," Rick said. "It just looks suspicious to me. I'm just asking you to be careful."

Carly just nodded at him, her mind troubled.

She left Rick at the front door to check out the security system while she ran upstairs to get dressed.

She couldn't help but think about what Rick had told her about his suspicions of Joe. Was Joe really the one breaking into her house? Thinking back over the last few days, she had to admit, he did act suspicious about some things. What was his fascination with the fireplace in the sitting room? Why was he so interested in the love letters between Vernon and Ruth? When they searched the house together, why was Joe so much more thorough about it than she was? What was he searching for? He had already lied to her about knowing Trinny. What else was he lying to her about. These questions and more plagued her mind as she got dressed.

Back downstairs, she watched as Rick finished resetting the codes on the security system. "Here's the new code," he told her. "I would advise not giving it to Joe this time. If the system has any problems, call me. I'll come over and check it out."

"No problem," Carly said.

"You ok?" Rick asked, noticing her sullen mood.

"Yeah, I'm fine. It's just hard to believe that Joe could be the person breaking into my house. I just don't want to believe it."

"I know. I understand. But if it walks like a duck and talks like a duck..."

"I know," Carly said on a long sigh. "Then it must be a duck."

"Carly, if you ever need me," Rick said, pulling her into his arms. "I'm here for you."

She raised her face to him and accepted his kiss eagerly. "I know you are. You seem to be my *knight in shining armor*."

"You bet I am."

After another long, heated kiss, Carly watched as Rick drove off down the driveway. She hated to see him go. Her mind wandered back to what Madam Hornbeck told her about following her heart. She knew now that her heart belonged to Rick. Lock, stock and barrel. She wasn't looking forward to the conversation she knew she would have to have with Joe, but she knew it was necessary. She couldn't keep leading him on knowing how she felt about Rick. And if he was her intruder, she certainly didn't want to get emotionally attached to him. Her suspicions of him were mounting.

She crawled into her car and headed toward the hospital. She was pushing it to get there right at ten the way the nurse had asked her to, but with everything that went on last night, she figured she had a good excuse for being a few minutes late this morning.

Asking for Vernon's room number at the information desk, she made her way to the fourth floor to find him.

He was sitting up in bed watching the local news when she walked in.

"Good morning, Vernon," she said, cheerily.

"You're late."

"Barely," she said, laying his clothes on the end of the bed. "It's only about quarter after."

"The nurse told you to be here at ten. What if they had discharged me at ten and you weren't here. Was I supposed to just sit in the lobby and wait for you?"

"Did they discharge you at ten?" Carly knew they hadn't and couldn't keep the sarcasm out of her voice.

"No, but they could have."

"What are you so grumpy about this morning, Vernon. Aren't you glad to be going home?"

"I ain't grumpy. I'm hungry," he grumbled. "The stuff they pass off as food in here is terrible."

"I'll swing by one of the fast food joints on the way home and grab you something."

"That stuff's even worse than what they serve in here," he said, looking at her like she was crazy. "I never touch that stuff. It'll kill you sooner than anything if you eat that junk."

Carly chuckled under her breath, but didn't say anything more about it. "I brought you some clothes," she said, indicating the pile at the end of his bed. "I hope they'll do."

Vernon grumbled something under his breath, but slowly got out of bed and examined the articles of clothing she had brought for him. "These'll do just fine." He picked up the stack of clothes and disappeared into the bathroom.

Several minutes later he emerged and went back over to the bed and sat down. "It wasn't easy getting dressed with only one arm," he said, accusingly.

"I don't imagine it was," Carly said. "If you needed help, all you had to do was ask."

"Hhmph..."

"Vernon," Carly said. "I need to talk to you. And I will not allow you to blow me off this time." Her voice was kind, but firm. She looked him directly in the eye waiting for his response.

"What do you want to talk about now?" he spat out at her.

Knowing he was still irritable, but also knowing it wasn't because of her, she dug around in her purse until she found the necklace she had tucked into one of the pockets and pulled it out.

Dangling it from her pointer finger right in front of his nose, she lifted her eyebrows at him and said, "Want to tell me about this?"

"Where'd you find that?" Vernon demanded, color rising in his cheeks. "You were snooping in my house, weren't you?"

"I found it draped over my aunt's urn in your closet," Carly told him. "I wasn't snooping. I was looking for a shirt for you and I saw it up on the shelf half hidden behind a box."

"Snooping," he spat out, nastily.

"You asked me to go into your house and get you some clothes. I did. It's not my fault if you had this sitting where I could see it. I didn't exactly go digging for it," Carly's temper was rising. She didn't appreciate being accused of snooping when she had been asked to go in there. "I think it's time you tell me about you and my aunt Ruth. No lies. No beating around the bush. The truth, Vernon. I want the truth."

Vernon looked at the necklace dangling from her finger and suddenly his shoulders drooped and he let out a long, deep sigh. "I bought that necklace for her years ago when we were young."

"I know you were her secret love," Carly said. "Can you tell me about it?"

"I don't really want to, but it seems you aren't going to let it rest, are you?" He didn't say this with a mean tone, but rather one of surrender.

"No," Carly said, gently. "I'm not going to let it go."

"Fine. But you need to promise me something first."

"What do you want me to promise?" Carly asked.

"That what I tell you will remain between you and me. I don't want you telling anyone else."

"Ok," Carly agreed. "I won't tell anyone, but you have to tell me the whole story. Not just bits and pieces."

"Agreed," Vernon said. Taking a deep breath, he began. "I came to the plantation when I was just a lad of about fifteen. I didn't have no formal education and knew I couldn't get a regular job. Ruth's dad hired me to keep up the grounds and to do the maintenance around the place, since I had a knack at doing things like that. I met Ruth shortly after I began working there. She was the most beautiful girl I'd ever seen, but I didn't think someone like her would ever be interested in me, so I went about my work and didn't bother her any. One day, she approached me in the gardens and started talking to me. One thing led to another and soon, we were meeting up behind the barn, out in the graveyard and just about anywhere we could that no one would see us."

He stopped and Carly noticed his eyes tearing up a little. She didn't want to hurt him with her questions, but she wanted to know more. "Go on, please," she said, when he didn't say anything else.

"I worked for two years to buy that necklace. It was all I had, money-wise. You see, working on a plantation back in those days didn't afford me a lot of money. I had to save for anything I wanted. So, one evening when I met Ruth up in the graveyard, I gave her that necklace as a sign of my affection. She gladly accepted it, but was afraid to wear it anytime other than when she was with me because if people saw her wearing a cheap piece of costume jewelry, they would know she was seeing someone who was beneath her social status. So I bought her that little box to keep it in when we weren't together. She would hide it under the floorboards in her room so her folks wouldn't find it. Eventually, she quit wearing it all together, but I know she still loved it…and me."

"She didn't want people to know she loved you just because you were of a different social standing than her?"

"That's right," Vernon said, sadly. "She was raised by her parents to believe that anyone in a lower class socially, was not acceptable to date or marry. She took on those beliefs, too. Oh, she loved me, but she wouldn't allow herself to be with me, except in private. I asked her once to marry me and she flat out refused. Told me she loved me, but could never marry me because I was a poor man and she was a rich woman and those two classes of people weren't meant to marry. I was heartbroken, but I figured it was better to have her secretly, than not have her at all. I loved that woman so much my heart hurt."

Carly leaned over and laid her hand on his arm. "I'm so sorry, Vernon. I just can't understand how she could believe that way. She obviously loved you."

"Oh, she did," Vernon said, with a smile on his face. "She told me I was her greatest treasure. When her folks died and the place became hers, she promised me I could always stay there and I would always have a job as long as I wanted it. She asked me to move into the carriage house, so I did. I couldn't have left if I'd wanted to. She was the love of my life and that plantation was the only home I've ever really known. She always told me that she would never leave that place because that's where her most treasured possession was...me. As long as I was at the plantation, she would never leave. So I never left either."

Carly's eyes welled up with tears and when she blinked, they rolled, unchecked, down her cheeks. "Oh Vernon," she said on a sob. "That's the most beautiful love story I've ever heard."

Vernon let the tears come. They rolled down his cheeks and he sniffled. "I still love her. That's why I keep her urn and that necklace in my room. I want her near me till it's my time to go."

"So," Carly said. "All the rumors of Aunt Ruth having a secret, hidden treasure somewhere around the place was true. But it wasn't gold or gems or some priceless object. It was *you*."

"Yes, I suppose that's right," Vernon said.

"Why don't you want anyone to know? Why do you want to keep it a secret?" Carly asked.

"Our whole relationship was a secret. Oh, there were rumors around town about her having a secret lover, but no one ever guessed or knew it was me. It was kind of fun for her and me to have out secret little relationship that we didn't have to share with anyone, but ourselves. I don't want to ruin that now. I want to honor her request to always let it be just between her and me."

Carly coiled the necklace into her hand and looked at it. Holding it out to Vernon, she said, "This belongs to you."

Vernon gingerly took the necklace out of her hand and wrapped it tightly in his fist. "Thank you," he said, softly.

"I know it was you who broke into the house the night the necklace disappeared,"

Carly told him gently. "Why didn't you just ask me for it?"

"I didn't want to have to explain all this to you," Vernon said, still clutching the necklace in his hand. "I just wanted to get it and keep it safe."

"Well, it's back where it belongs now," Carly said, leaning over and squeezing his hand.

"Can I keep her ashes? I know they rightfully belong to you, but I was hoping..."

"Of course, you can," Carly said. "I think they belong more to you than to me anyway."

Vernon nodded, but didn't say anything.

"Um, Vernon?" Carly asked. "You didn't happen to break into the house on any other occasion, did you?"

"No, why?"

"Someone's been coming into the house during the night. I have no idea why, or what they're looking for, but it's happened a couple of times now."

"Weren't me, missy. I only came in the one time to get the necklace."

About that time, the nurse came in holding a clipboard full of papers. "Time for you to go home, Mr. Knowles," she said. "I just need you sign these papers and you're a free man."

"You're late," Vernon told the nurse. "You said I'd be released at ten."

"We're running a bit behind this morning, Mr. Knowles, but better late than never, right?" the nurse asked in good humor.

"I suppose," he grumbled at her, though he turned his head toward Carly and winked.

Carly put her head down and chuckled. She was starting to learn that Vernon's bark was worse than his bite.

Carly waited for the nurse to finish with Vernon's at-home care instructions, then left to go bring the car around to the front of the hospital to wait for the nurse to wheel Vernon down to her.

The drive home was pleasant. Vernon seemed to be in a much better mood than when she had first gotten to the hospital. Carly assumed it was a burden off his shoulders to finally be able to tell someone about his long held secret.

Carly was growing very fond of Vernon. She was beginning to realize that his grumpy attitude was simply just part of who he was. She decided not to take it personally anymore when he acted that way toward her.

After getting Vernon situated in his arm chair and setting his medications out where he could get to them easily, Carly walked back to the house.

She still had most of the day to find something to do until Joe returned late this afternoon or evening. She didn't know exactly when to expect him, but she needed something to do to occupy her mind. She was driving herself crazy with all the thoughts running through her head. What would he do when she told him she didn't want to see him anymore? Would he hurt her as Trinny had suggested someone might? Or would he just agree, since they seemed to butt heads so often.

Carly felt a small prick of sadness touch her heart. She had really thought she liked Joe, but now, she was thinking it had probably been more along the lines of lust. Undeniably, he was good looking, but looks weren't everything, right?

Her mind wandered to Rick. Rick was handsome, funny and easy to be around. They didn't spend a lot of time arguing or fussing over things, either. She couldn't deny the feeling of warmth that spread through her when she was wrapped in his arms. The closest thing she could relate it to was *home*. He felt like *home*.

Not wanting to dwell on her upcoming confrontation with Joe, she decided to retrace her steps from last night and see if she could find any clues as to who was in her house and what they were looking for.

Entering the sitting room, she walked straight to the fireplace. She ran her hands all along the tile that surrounded it, looking for any clue as to why Trinny would lead her here, then just disappear into it.

The tiles held no clues, so she dropped to her knees and looked around the inside of the fireplace. Nothing immediately caught her attention, but when she started to pull her head out, she noticed small scrape marks on the floor under the grate.

She pulled on the grate, but it wouldn't budge. It was welded onto a small metal plate that sat on the floor of the fireplace. She pulled and tugged on the grate hoping the metal plate would move, but it remained where it was. Giving up, she dusted off her hands and sat back on her knees.

What caused the scratch marks on the floor of the fireplace? Wood being shuffled around? Not likely. These marks were scratched into a metal floor. Wood wouldn't scrape metal like that.

Shifting her legs, she accidentally pulled the rug back from under her and once again noticed the scratch marks on the floor, just under the corner of the rug.

Something was leaving scratch marks on the floor and in the fireplace, but what?

Not finding any clues around the fireplace, she stood up and looked at the bookcases.

"Hhhmmm," she said out loud. "In the movies, there's always a book that when pulled out, triggers a hidden doorway. Could it really be that easy?"

She began pulling each book out by its bindings, but none of them unlocked a secret doorway.

She looked at the fireplace and the bookcases and stomped her foot. "Come on!" she demanded. "Give up your secrets."

Nothing happened.

She huffed out her breath and decided to go check out the attic.

Before she headed up the stairs, she made a quick detour to the kitchen for the carving knife. She didn't want to go up there without something to defend herself with. What if someone was up there again? She knew she was freaking herself out, but she grabbed the knife anyway and headed up the stairs.

Once she reached the attic, she flipped the lights on and looked around. The pile of boxes she had been under the night before still lay in disarray just down the aisle to the left. She looked behind her toward the other end of the room and noticed dusty foot tracks leading back into the darkness. It was hard to tell the size of the foot tracks or whether they were male or female sized due to the fact that they were scuffed around as if the person leaving them didn't want anyone to know what size or sex they belonged to.

Following them, she saw that they turned off the center aisle and stopped at a stack of boxes which had all been opened and their contents scattered across the floor.

Old clothing, knick knacks and odds and ends of junk lay piled all around.

Carly dug through the contents laying on the floor, but nothing of value was among the items. She flipped open boxes that were stacked next to the discarded items, but still, nothing but junk, filled them.

Turning to leave, she noticed that even an old dresser had had its drawers pulled out and tossed aside. She wondered if that had been one of the thumps she had heard last night, when one of the drawers had hit the floor.

There was no doubt about it. Someone was searching for something, but what? All these boxes were filled with was nothing but old memorabilia and junk.

She took one more look around the room, but other than a few boxes and an old dresser, nothing else seemed to be disturbed. She must have disturbed the intruder before he or she could complete their search.

She climbed back down the ladder and shut the attic door.

She could still see the small, smeared soot stain on the door. How did soot get on the attic door? What was the connection?

Shaking her head, she headed back downstairs to wait for Joe.

Chapter 21

Joe called later that afternoon and told her he would be over once he showered and changed clothes.

Carly's nerves were on edge. She hated confrontations, but knew she couldn't avoid this one.

An hour later, she heard his pickup pull up in front of the house. Wiping her sweaty palms on the front of her jeans, she opened the front door to Joe's knock.

"Hey," he said as he stepped inside. He reached out to pull her into a hug, but she stepped back out of his reach.

She saw the questioning look on his face and felt bad, but she didn't want to give him the impression everything was alright.

"Hi," she said. "Have a good trip?"

Joe noticed her cool demeanor and looked at her quizzically. "Is something wrong?" he asked.

"Why don't I get some coffee ready, then we can talk," Carly said.

"Oookkkk," Joe said, slowly.

She turned on her heel and headed down the hallway toward the kitchen.

Joe pulled a bar stool up to the island and waited patiently for Carly to put the coffee on.

When it was finished brewing, she poured two cups, setting one in from of him and keeping one for herself.

Pulling up a seat across the island from him, she took a sip of her coffee before she spoke. "How well did you know Trinny?" she asked, trying to keep her voice even. She was watching him closely, trying to gauge his reactions.

"Why? What's this all about, Carly? What's going on?" He didn't seem angry, just a little irritated.

"I asked you a question, Joe. How...well...did...you...know...Trinny?" She paused between each word to add emphasis to her question.

"I'm guessing you found out that I dated her," Joe said. It wasn't a question, but rather a statement.

"Why did I have to find out through someone else? Why didn't you tell me?" Carly asked. "It should have come from you, Joe."

"I didn't want you to know because I figured if you knew, you wouldn't want to date me yourself."

"So lying to me was better?"

"I was going to tell you eventually. It didn't last long between her and me."

"Was she the old girlfriend you didn't want me to see in the photo on your mantle?"

"Yes," Joe said. "Let me explain, please."

"You'd better," Carly said. She could feel her anger rising, but didn't want to start a fight. She had too many things she wanted to ask him first.

"I met her shortly after she started working for your aunt. We hit it off almost immediately. I asked her out and she agreed, so we began dating. Everything was going great until one day, she just up and left. I came over to see her and Ruth told me she had packed up several valuable items and skipped town. I never saw her again. She never even told me goodbye."

"That's because she's dead, Joe," Carly said, flatly. "She didn't just leave town."

"There's no proof of that," Joe said. "No body has ever been found."

"I've been seeing her ghost. You know that."

"You claim to see her ghost, but I've never seen it. Even the time in the cemetery that you claimed she was standing behind me or the time you said she flew between us, I never saw her. Only you did. Maybe you're imagining things."

"I didn't imagine it, Joe," Carly ground out. "She's here. She's haunting this place. She's real."

"Whatever you say, Carly." Joe just shook his head and took a drink of his coffee.

Carly was so irritated, she wanted to strangle him. "Are you still in love with her? Is that why you took such a sudden interest in me? Because I look so much like her? I remind you of her?"

"Maybe. I don't know," Joe said. "The first day I met you, I have to admit, I was shocked at the similarities between the two of you. You look so much like her. Maybe I did see her in you at that point, but then, after we started spending time together, I really began to like you for yourself, not because you reminded me of her."

"Gee, how sweet," Carly said sarcastically. "I almost fell for you."

"Almost?" Joe asked. "Seems to me you fell pretty hard for me."

"I thought I had, too, but now I realize it was just lust. I'm not in love with you and I never was."

"Keep telling yourself that if it helps," Joe said, drinking more of his coffee.

His smugness was infuriating. Carly was beginning to see a side of him that was very unflattering. What did Trinny ever see in him?

"Have you been breaking into my house?" Carly asked him, bluntly.

"What?" Joe asked. "No. Why would I break into your house?"

"Well someone has been and it seems awful convenient that it happened again last night while you were supposedly out of town. Where were you really, Joe? Snooping around my house?"

"Oh, for heaven's sake, Carly. I was picking up supplies out of town for the job I have coming up next week. I told you that."

"You left town without even telling me. Then, when I tried calling you after someone attacked me in the attic, you never answered your phone and you never called me back. Seems pretty suspicious to me."

"You were attacked last night? In the attic?" Joe asked. "Didn't the alarm go off warning you that someone was in the house?"

"No, it didn't. But then again, you did have the codes, didn't you? Another coincidence? Why didn't you answer your phone or call me back? It was because you were in my house and if you had answered your phone, I would have heard you," Carly accused him.

"I didn't have any cell service. I never got your call, Carly."

"Right," Carly said, clearly not believing him. "How convenient."

"I never broke into your house. Why would I?"

"You tell me," Carly demanded angrily. "Looking back, you've acted rather suspiciously at times."

"Like when?" Joe asked.

"What's your fascination with the fireplace in the sitting room? I found you staring at it that one day."

"I'm a carpenter. I love the detail it has and was impressed with how it was made."

"What about your interest in my aunt's and Vernon's love letters? Why would you care about those?" Carly asked.

"Who wouldn't be? It was interesting to find out about the two of them, that's all."

"When we were searching the house after the one break-in, you seemed to be searching much harder than I was. What were you looking for?" Carly asked.

"I was helping you search for anything that might be missing. Really, Carly? This is what you're basing your accusations on? Because I was being thorough when I was helping you out? You're being a bit paranoid, don't you think?"

"I'm not being paranoid, Joe. Someone's breaking into my house and searching for something. I just don't know what it is they're looking for."

"Well, it's not me," Joe said, exasperated.

"I don't want to see you anymore," Carly said. "It's over between us."

"Whatever," Joe said, curling his lip up. "Good luck finding anyone as good as me. I treated you real good, Carly."

"You treated me real good?" Carly asked, completely flabbergasted. "What, by lying to me? By calling me paranoid and not believing me when I told you I've been seeing Trinny? Yeah, that's being real good to me alright."

"You'll miss me. Just wait and see."

"I won't miss you, Joe," Carly said. "Rick is more of a man than you'll ever be."

"Rick, huh?" Joe asked, scooting his chair back and standing up. "So, you've been canoodling around with him behind my back, have you? I should have known."

"You need to leave," Carly said, getting up from her seat. "And don't bother ever coming back here. You won't be welcome."

"No problem," Joe said, storming down the hallway. "But you'll be sorry, Carly. Mark my words."

Carly followed him down the hallway to the front door.

Joe grabbed the doorknob and gave it a sharp turn, then threw the door open and stepped out onto the veranda. Just as he was turning around to say something more to her, Carly slammed the door in his face and slipped the lock loudly into place.

Leaning against the door, she closed her eyes and let out a long sigh.

That had not gone as she had hoped. She didn't want to make an enemy of him, but things just went from bad to worse.

Should she believe his flimsy excuses about his suspicious behavior? She wanted to believe him. Even though he turned out to be a real jerk, she still hoped it wasn't him breaking into her house. She didn't want to believe it had been someone she thought had been a friend.

Pushing herself off the door, she peeked outside to make sure he was gone, then seeing that his truck was nowhere in sight, she walked around the side of the house to go check on Vernon.

Vernon seemed pleased to see her. He opened the door and welcomed her in.

"How are you doing?" she asked him, taking a seat on his couch.

"Oh, I'm fine," he said. "You ok?"

"Yeah," Carly said on a sigh. "I just ended things with Joe."

"Good," Vernon said. "I never liked that guy."

"You didn't? Why?"

"Never trusted him," Vernon said. "He was always so uppity and thought too much of himself, if you ask me. After Ruth died, he was always snooping around the place and roaming the property like he owned it."

"He told me he was keeping an eye on things. He figured you weren't capable of handling things if someone came around causing trouble," Carly said. "Do you think he could be the one breaking into the house?"

Vernon scrunched up his face as if he was thinking really hard. "Don't know, but I suppose it's possible."

"Why would he, though? What would he be looking for?" Carly asked.

"No idea, missy. I'm not saying it's him. Just because I don't like him, don't make him a criminal."

"Well, I suppose that's true. Did you know he used to date Trinny?"

"Sure," Vernon said. "Though I never understood what she saw in him."

Carly laughed. "I was wondering the same thing."

They talked for awhile and Carly was beginning to relax. She had been all stressed out and tense after her fight with Joe and sitting here talking to Vernon felt good.

A thought came to her when she looked over at his fireplace. "Do you know anything about the fireplace in the sitting room?"

"Like what?"

"Oh, I don't know," Carly said, feeling silly. "Joe seemed to have a fascination with it, and last night, Trinny led me to it, then just floated into it and disappeared."

"It's been a part of the house since I've been here. It wasn't added or restored to my knowledge. You say Trinny led you to it?"

"Yes, she got me out of bed and took me to the sitting room, then just disappeared into the fireplace and never came back out."

"I've only seen her a couple of times," Vernon said. "Both times was up in the cemetery. Your aunt used to tell me she saw her often, but could never figure out what she wanted."

"I wish I knew," Carly said. "I'll just have to keep trying to communicate with her."

"Eventually, you'll figure it out," Vernon said, yawning.

"You must be tired," Carly said, getting to her feet. "Let me get you your meds and I'll go."

She set his meds on the table next to his chair and prepared to leave.

"Carly," Vernon said. "Be careful, will you?"

"Sure," Carly said.

"I'm serious, missy. Something ain't right and you know it."

"I do know it," Carly said. "But Rick is keeping an eye on me and I know that if I need him, he'll be here."

"Rick's a good man," Vernon said. "Born and raised in these parts. Been with the Sheriff's office for several years now. You call him if anything else strange goes on, you hear?"

"I will, Vernon," Carly said. "Good night."

Carly let herself out so Vernon wouldn't have to get up.

Closing the door behind her, she saw that the sun was almost set and the darkening sky was splashing reds, yellows and oranges in streaks across the horizon.

Taking in a deep breath of the fragrant night air, she stepped off the porch and onto the stone path that led to the house.

Just as she took the first step, a sound reached her ears.

It was the sound of her name, floating to her on a gentle breeze.

Cccaaarrrlllyyy..."

Turning her head toward the sound, she saw Trinny at the foot of the hill that led to the cemetery.

Her long, dark hair hanging limply over her shoulders. Her dirty, stained nightgown flowing around her legs. A soft, ethereal glow emanating from around her.

Slowly she lifted her arm and beckoned Carly to her.

"Cccooommmeee..." she said. Her voice barely audible.

Carly took a step toward her as Trinny turned and floated up the hill toward the cemetery.

Chapter 22

Carly followed the ghostly form of her sister as she floated over the ground up the hill.

Once they reached the top, Trinny continued her trek, drifting effortlessly as she passed gravestone after gravestone until she reached the tall spire of Rutherford Montgomery's headstone.

Carly stood on the path in front of the marker and stared at it. Here she was again, in front of the headstone that always seemed to draw her.

She couldn't seem to pull her eyes away from it. Her gaze followed it from the tip of the spire all the way down to the flat, square base.

Trinny's misty form floated up to her and her white, translucent arm reached out for Carly's hand.

Carly felt a bone deep chill soak into her hand and arm. The sudden temperature change caused her to look toward the source.

Trinny was touching her hand, but it wasn't a physical touch. Carly could see the ghostly hand on her, but couldn't feel the pressure of it or a warmth coming from it. Instead, the sensation was like the chilling cold of an icy wind, brushing over her skin.

Shocked out of her hypnotic stare of the gravestone, Carly looked up into Trinny's face.

Trinny's beautiful green eyes seemed to pierce clear through Carly. Blinking several times, she reached her hand up to touch Trinny's face.

"What happened to you?" she whispered to her, as a deep sadness filled her.

Trinny's eyes turned sad, but she didn't say anything. Carly knew it was taking a lot of her energy to appear to her and stay with her as long as she had. So, instead of trying to get her to talk, she simply laid her hand on top of Trinny's and asked, "What are you trying to show me?"

Trinny wafted around to the back of the gravestone and pointed down at the square, flat base. Carly followed her around and stared at the spot she was indicating. There, right where Trinny was pointing, was the scuff marks Carly had seen before. She reached out and traced them with her fingertips.

Trinny lifted her spectral hands and laid them against the base of the stone. Carly watched her do this, but wasn't sure what it meant.

"Trinny, what does that mean?" she asked, watching her sister repeatedly lift her hands and place them on the base of the stone.

"Push," Trinny murmured softly.

Carly looked at where Trinny was placing her hands and placed her own in the same spot. She pushed the stone, but nothing happened. She looked at Trinny, but Trinny only nodded back.

Carly leaned into the stone again and pushed harder.

It moved.

Carly jumped back and stared at the gravestone.

Looking back at Trinny, she saw that she was smiling at her and nodding rapidly. Her misty form was beginning to slightly fade, then would become clearer again. Carly knew she would have to hurry or Trinny could disappear completely.

Bracing her shoulder against the stone, Carly pushed with all her might. The stone groaned, but slowly slid forward. With each inch it moved, it made a soft scraping noise. Carly looked down and saw what had made the scuff marks on the stone. It was the base of the gravestone as it slid across its own base.

Inch by inch, Carly pushed the stone forward until it wouldn't move any farther. She looked down at the base and saw a narrow hole open up that dropped down into darkness.

Trinny leaned over the hole and looking up at Carly, pointed down into the darkness below.

"You want me to go down there?" Carly asked, stunned.

Trinny nodded and floated up over the hole and suddenly dropped down into it out of sight.

"Oh brother," Carly said, suddenly feeling very nervous. "What have I gotten myself into?"

A faint, otherworldly glow filled the void below where Trinny had just disappeared down into.

Carly leaned over and looked down into the hole. A wooden ladder was leaning up against the wall just below the opening.

Turning around, Carly lowered one foot at a time onto the ladder. Step by step she sunk deeper into the black hole.

Several steps down, she took one more step and felt earth beneath her foot. Breathing a sigh of relief, she turned to find a deep, black hole stretching out before her.

A tunnel.

There was a tunnel under Rutherford Montgomery's headstone.

Looking around for Trinny's ghostly illumine, she realized her sister was gone.

"Trinny?" Carly called out. "Where are you? Please don't leave me now."

A faint glow appeared several feet in front of her. "I'm here, Carly."

"Please don't leave me down here alone," Carly pleaded.

"I will stay with you," Trinny said, barely above a whisper.

Trinny turned and slowly drifted down the tunnel. She went at a slow pace, so it was easy for Carly to keep up.

The tunnel was formed out of packed dirt. The floor was bumpy and uneven as if hundreds of feet over the years had trod over it, breaking down the soil in spots. The walls were hard packed dirt that was cold to the touch. No lights lit up the passageway. No handrails adorned the walls to help guide those who dared venture down here. A dank, earthy smell filled the place and the air was chilly and damp, raising goosebumps on Carly's skin. It was a very rough, crude passageway meant to offer undetected movement of people from one location to another.

Carly wondered where the other end came out. She had an uneasy feeling in the pit of her stomach that told her she already knew the answer to that.

As they made their way deeper into the tunnel, the ground began to slope downwards.

Wet spots on the earthen floor caused by water seeping into the tunnel from small cracks in the walls, made walking in certain spots slippery and dangerous.

Carly picked her way along, walking cautiously, not knowing what might be up head or around the next bend. Trinny's luminescence was the only light she had to see her way through the dark tunnel.

They walked on for what seemed like a long time when Trinny suddenly stopped.

The ground had leveled out again and Carly could see that Trinny was hovering over top of something.

Carly stepped up next to her and her toe kicked something solid. Jumping back, she looked down to see what she had kicked.

Trinny's ghostly glow was softly lighting up the area where they were standing and Carly looked down to see a skeleton curled up in a small cutout along the wall. The bones were wrapped in a ragged, stained white piece of cloth that at one time had been a nightgown. Black strands of hair hung in grotesque clumps across the dull, yellowed skull. Next to the skeleton was a canvas bag tied with a strand of twine.

Carly gasped and jumped backward, trying to get away from the horrible sight. Her gaze jumped to Trinny and her blood ran cold and seemed to freeze in her veins.

Trinny stared down at the skeleton, a forlorn, sad expression on her spectral face.

Carly's heart sank.

So, this is where Trinny had been all this time. Her body lay broken and decaying in the bottom of a long forgotten tunnel.

"Oh, Trinny," Carly said. She could hardly get the words out. "This is what you've been trying to tell me, isn't it. You wanted me to find your body."

Trinny slowly nodded and looked up at Carly. "Please," she said, her voice barely a whisper. "Bury me, Carly. Don't let my body rest down here forever."

Carly looked at the body of what used to be her sister. A deep sadness welled up inside of her. Tears began to run down her cheeks as she looked back up at Trinny. "Of course," she said. "I'll give you a proper burial, Trinny."

Trinny floated around the room while Carly considered how to get her sister's remains out of the tunnel.

Staring down at the bones, Carly noticed something around the neck. Leaning down, she gently grabbed the silky material between her fingers and lifted it up to get a better look.

A scarf.

Suddenly, realization dawned on her. Jerking her head in Trinny's direction, she indicated the scarf she now held in her hand.

"Trinny," she said, her voice trembling. "Someone killed you, didn't they? You didn't steal Aunt Ruth's stuff and run away. Someone killed you and dumped you down here." She could hardly breathe. Her hand was shaking as she held the scarf out toward Trinny. "They used this to strangle you."

Trinny's ghostly hand reached out and touched the scarf. "Yes, I was murdered."

"Why were you murdered? Who killed you, Trinny?" Carly asked, afraid of the answer. "Who did this to you? Was it Joe?"

Trinny's head jerked up and her mouth flew open, but no sound came out. She raised her pale, white arm and pointed behind Carly.

Carly spun around as she heard footsteps approaching from behind her.

Suddenly, she was cast into total darkness.

Swinging around, she realized that Trinny had vanished, taking with her the only light Carly had.

Carly dug around in her pocket for her phone and clicked on the flashlight app. Aiming it down the tunnel, she began to see a shadowy form coming toward her.

"Whose there?" she cried out.

Suddenly a dark shape stepped into the light cast by her phone.

Joe.

Carly sucked in her breath and took a step backward, almost tripping over Trinny's remains.

"It was you," Carly growled out at him. "You killed my sister."

Joe just looked at her and shook his head slowly from side to side.

Out of the darkness, a voice drifted up from behind Joe. "He sure seems the type, doesn't he?"

Carly squinted, trying to see who had spoken. Her nerves were on end and fear creeped up her spine.

Joe suddenly cringed and his body jerked forward and he went sprawling across the floor. He landed face down with a thud next to her.

Carly screamed and stepped back, tripping over the skeleton and falling backward onto the ground next to the unconscious Joe.

"He'll be so easy to pin this all on," the voice said from out of the shadows.

Carly lifted her phone and shown it in the direction of the voice.

Suddenly, the man behind the voice stepped out of the shadows and into the light from Carly's phone.

Rick.

Carly's heart began to beat so fast, she couldn't breathe.

"Rick?" she asked, unbelieving. "Rick, what's this all about?"

She started to get to her feet, but Rick took a step closer to her and by the maniacal look in his eyes, she knew she was in danger, so she remained where she was.

"I can't believe you didn't figure it out, Carly," Rick sneered. "You're not as smart I as thought you were."

"Figure what out? What are you talking about?" Carly asked.

"Poor Joe," Rick snarled. "He's actually innocent, but it was so easy to convince you that he was the one breaking into your house."

"It was you?" Carly asked, stunned. "But why? What are you looking for?"

"Why, the hidden treasure, of course. I grew up hearing all the tales coming from this place. All about Ruth's hidden treasure. Your aunt used to tell my mom that she would never leave this place. That her treasure was here. So, I made it my mission to find that treasure. Why should Ruth get to have it all? She had this big, fancy house, a small fortune in the bank. Why did she need anything more? She needed to share the wealth a little bit."

"Rick, there is no treasure," Carly said. "Her treasure was..."

"Don't lie to me!" Rick shouted at her. "Of course there's a treasure. Everyone heard your aunt talking about her secret treasure for years."

"Rick..."

Rick pulled his arm out from behind his back and pointed a gun at her face.

Carly gasped and threw her hands up to protect herself.

"I've been searching your wretched house for years trying to find where it's hidden. I'm running out of places to look, so I was hoping that when you moved in, you might find it for me, but all you were concerned with was Joe." He waved the pistol toward Joe, then pointed it back at Carly again.

"Rick, there is no treasure. Please let me explain," Carly said. But Rick didn't let her finish.

"You know how I found this tunnel? The library. My mom told me a few years back that the blueprints for some of the old mansions around the area are kept on file there. It didn't take long for me to dig them up. Once I found out about this tunnel, I knew it was the perfect way to get in and out of the house without being detected. Well almost..."

"Almost?" Carly asked, afraid to hear what he was going to say.

"I was sneaking into the house late one night like I'd done a hundred times before, but this one time, I was caught. Your sister," he spat out the words, "heard a noise and came to investigate. She caught me coming out of the fireplace entrance. I couldn't let her get away, could I?"

Carly looked down at the skeleton laying on the ground next to her. "You're sick, Rick. You need help."

Rick ignored her. "She was going to rat me out. Tell your aunt about me. Call the cops. I couldn't let that happen. When she turned away from me to go get help, I grabbed a silk scarf that was laying on the back of the couch and I flung it around her neck and squeezed. I squeezed and squeezed until she stopped fighting. Once I knew she was dead, I stopped. But I couldn't leave the body there in the sitting room, so I dragged her down here and dumped her. No one would ever find her here because no one else knew about the tunnel. Just me. I don't think your aunt even knew about it. I needed to make it look like Trinny left town on her own, so I grabbed up a few of Ruth's valuables and stuffed them in a bag I had with me and tossed them into the tunnel along with her. I started up the rumor about her stealing from your aunt and leaving town. All I had to do was tell my mom and soon, the whole town would hear about it. Everyone seemed to buy it, so that became the story of why she suddenly disappeared. Brilliant, huh?"

Carly stared at him. He was a monster. How had she not seen it? How could he hide this evil, ugly side of himself from her?

"You see, Carly. I deserve the treasure. Why should I live month to month on my meager cop salary while your aunt was living with so much wealth? That's not very fair, now is it?"

"You set up the security system for me because you knew it wouldn't go off. You never came through one of the doors or windows. You always came in through this tunnel," Carly said, flatly.

"That's right," Rick said. "By me putting in the security system, it would throw suspicion away from me. That's why I gave you my personal phone number, too. After the first time you called the cops and I was dispatched out, I saw an opportunity. I didn't want you calling the cops every time you heard a strange noise. I figured by giving you my number, I could show up and not involve the sheriff's department at all. I didn't want them snooping around and finding any evidence that might lead back to me."

"It was you in the attic, too, wasn't it. You were the one who attacked me," Carly said.

"It was me every time," Rick said. "Whenever I would sneak into the house, I would park my truck just down the road a piece. That way, I could make a quick getaway if I needed to and it proved helpful the night you came up into the attic. I heard you coming, so I hid behind those boxes, but you saw me. It was so convenient that those boxes were stacked there. One good push and down they went. I knew you could have gotten out from under them easily enough, so the dresser presented itself as a tool to keep you down long enough for me to get away."

"You tried to kill me," Carly accused.

"No, just deter you long enough to get away," Rick said. "I wasn't done with you. You hadn't led me to the treasure yet."

"If you were so close, why did it take you so long to get to me once I called you," Carly asked.

"Because," Rick said. "I had to get out of the house and back to my truck so I could quickly change clothes and rest for a minute so that when I finally got to you, you wouldn't see the ski mask I was wearing, or hear me panting. I knew you would be ok till I got back. I wasn't ready for you to die yet."

"Rick, there is no treasure," Carly said. "The treasure was Vernon. I found love letters between them. Vernon is the one who broke into the house the first time. He stole a necklace I found under the floorboards in my bedroom that he had given to my aunt. When I confronted him about it, he told me that they had a secret relationship for years and that he was her secret treasure. She would never leave this place as long as he was here."

"No," Rick said. "No, that's not true. There's a treasure buried here somewhere and I'm going to find it."

Joe began to stir on the ground next to her. Carly reached out and laid her hand on his back. "Rick, he's hurt. He needs a doctor."

"He'll be fine. He shouldn't have been here in the first place, so it's his fault I had to drag him down here and pistol whip him."

"What do you mean?" Carly asked.

"I was perched out in the cemetery waiting for my chance to sneak back into the house tonight when I saw you come up the hill. I watched as you pushed the stone back exposing the tunnel. Frankly, I was shocked you knew about it. Then shortly after you went down the hole, I see good old Joe here coming along the path from his place. I assumed he was heading for your house, but he saw me crouched behind a headstone. He asked me what I was doing, so I shoved my gun in his face and brought him down into the tunnel with me. It worked out in my favor though, cause now, he'll be framed to make it look like he killed Trinny and you, then turned the gun on himself. I've got it all planned out."

Carly felt sick to her stomach. She looked around, but Trinny had not reappeared.

"I wasn't alone in the cemetery. Trinny was with me," she said.

Rick scoffed at her. "Sure she was. Seems to me, Trinny is right where I left her." He pointed to the pile of bones on the floor.

"You're not going to get away with this. Someone will find out you did it," Carly said.

"Really?" Rick asked. "No one suspects me of doing anything wrong. Even you thought I was innocent. You were so ready to pin it all on Joe, too."

Joe began to stir again. Rick walked up to him and straddled him. Looking wickedly at Carly, he brought the butt of his gun down hard on the top of Joe's head. Joe slumped to the ground again and made no further move to get up.

"Time to go into the house now, Carly," Rick said. "You're going to show me where the treasure is."

"Rick, I told you," Carly said. "There is no treasure."

Rick backhanded her, knocking her sideways onto the skeleton of Trinny.

"Stop your lying, right now," Rick yelled. "My mom has heard all the rumors about this place and has passed each and every one of them on to me. Your aunt told my mom on several occasions that she wouldn't leave this place because of her treasure. You honestly expect me to believe that a grumpy, old man was her treasure? Please. Don't take me for a fool."

Rick reached down and grabbed Joe by the scruff of his collar and hoisted his torso off the ground. Waving the gun at Carly, he motioned for her to walk ahead of him.

Carly climbed to her feet and, using her phone for light, made her way deeper down the tunnel.

Rick followed closely behind, dragging Joe by the collar as he went. Joe's lifeless body hung limp in his hands, his feet bumping along over the uneven ground.

After walking for several minutes, Rick called up to her, "Stop," he said. "Turn your light to the left. There's a small door there. Push it open and crawl through."

Carly shone her light to the left and saw a small metal door situated in the earthen wall. Feeling her way over it's surface, she found a small handle. Gripping it and using her shoulder to push, the small metal door slid open. As it moved, it made a very familiar scraping sound.

She knew now that this was the noise she kept hearing late at night. It was a small hidden doorway that went from the tunnel into the fireplace in the sitting room.

Once the door was opened all the way, Rick shoved her in the back and said, "Get in there. If you try to run once you're through, I'll shoot you before you can even get across the room."

Carly crawled through the small opening and out through the fireplace and into the sitting room. She saw that the door swung out from the fireplace and over the floor in front of it, just barely scraped across the top of it where the area rug lay.

Turning, she saw Rick hoist Joe up and shove him partway through the hole. "Grab him, Carly," Rick demanded. "Pull him through."

Carly grabbed Joe under his arms and pulled him the rest of the way into the room.

Rick squeezed through the hole and closed the secret door behind him, returning the fireplace to it's normal appearance. The little door undetectable to the untrained eye.

Grabbing Joe by the collar again, he dragged him across the room and dropped him in front of the couch.

Pulling out a long cord of rope from his pocket, Rick tied Joe's hands and feet together and then wrapped the rope around the leg of the couch several times to keep Joe from being able to move should he wake up.

Pointing his gun at Carly, he said, "Now, where's the treasure?"

Chapter 23

Carly stared down the barrel of the gun. "I told you, Rick. There is no treasure."

Rick's hand darted out and he grabbed a handful of Carly's hair. Jerking her up, he shoved her toward the door and into the foyer. "I'm only going to ask you one more time. Where's...the...treasure?"

Carly winced in pain as he jerked her around by her hair.

As they entered the foyer, Carly looked over and saw Trinny's apparition through the window that was beside the front door. Trinny's voice filled Carly's head, though her words were not spoken out loud. "Take him to the cemetery, Carly."

Carly didn't waste time trying to figure out exactly what Trinny meant. She trusted her sister to lead her in the right direction.

Instead, she lifted her arm and pointed to the door. "Ok, ok. It's out there," she said. "It's in the cemetery."

"What do you mean it's in the cemetery?" Rick asked, yanking her head back so he could look down into her face.

Trying to come up with something quickly, she said the first thing that came to her mind. "It's buried in the cemetery."

"Where?" Rick demanded. "Where in the cemetery?"

"In one of the graves."

"Which one?"

"I'll have to show you when we get up there. I don't remember the name on it."

Seemingly satisfied with her answer, Rick wound her hair tightly around his fist and moved her toward the door.

"I see you didn't set the alarm," he said, as he turned the knob on the front door and swung it open. "What good does it do if you don't turn it on?" He laughed as he shoved her out onto the veranda.

Carly grabbed the fist that he had her hair in with both her hands, trying to keep him from him yanking on it so much. "I was only going to see Vernon. I didn't think to set it."

"Stupid girl," Rick said.

Carly looked to the end of the veranda and saw Trinny standing there waiting for them to walk around the side of the house.

As they rounded the end of the house, Trinny floated on ahead to the bottom of the hill that led up to the cemetery.

Carly kept her eyes on Trinny as they made their way to the foot of the hill.

Was Trinny leading them to a specific grave? She didn't want to lose sight of her. Maybe she knew something Carly didn't.

They finally reached the top of the hill and Rick stopped and looked around. "Which way?" he asked.

Carly looked around for Trinny and saw her standing next to a grave a couple of rows behind Rutherford Montgomery's headstone.

"There," Carly said, pointing to where Trinny was standing.

Carly knew Rick couldn't see Trinny. She didn't know why Trinny was keeping herself hidden from Rick, but she wasn't going to tell Rick that she was there. Trinny must have her reasons for not showing herself to him.

They made their way across the graveyard, stepping over graves and weaving between stones.

When Carly reached the grave that Trinny was hovering over, she told Rick to stop. "It's here," she said.

Rick looked around like he was looking for something. "What am I supposed to dig with?"

"There's a shovel in the lawn shed down by the carriage house," Carly told him.

Rick pulled more rope out of his pocket and had Carly lay on the ground next to the grave while he bound her hands and feet together.

He tightened the ropes to the point the fibers were digging into her skin. She winced in pain, but Rick showed no concern. "Now you stay here like a good little girl, while I go get a shovel."

Carly watched as he trotted off across the cemetery and disappeared down the hill.

"Trinny?" Carly whispered. "Are you still here?"

"Trinny's misty, white form appeared at her side. "Yes, Carly. I'm here," she said.

"What do I do now? There's no treasure here."

"Have him dig a deep hole on the backside of the grave and leave the rest to me," Trinny said.

It was dark outside, except for the light of the moon, which cast a soft, eerie haze over the land. There was just enough light being cast to see what you were doing without needing a flashlight.

Carly heard, rather than saw, Rick returning. His footfalls were coming hard and fast.

He stepped up next to Carly and hauling her into a sitting position, leaned her back up against a headstone next to the one Trinny indicated for her to have him dig at.

"Ok, Carly," Rick said, leaning on the shovel handle as he spoke to her. "Where do I dig?"

"On the back side of that grave you're standing next to," she told him. She hoped her voice sounded believable, because inside, she was trembling and terrified and she was afraid he'd see right through her lie.

Rick grabbed up the shovel and jammed it into the ground behind the headstone. He lifted several shovelfuls of dirt out of the hole he was digging, when he stopped and looked over at Carly. "How deep is it? I should have hit something by now."

Trinny leaned down and whispered in Carly's ear, "Tell him it's really deep so someone couldn't easily find it."

"It's buried really deep," Carly said, following Trinny's instructions. "Aunt Ruth didn't want someone to find it so she made sure it was buried deep. You'll have to dig several feet down."

Rick looked at her skeptically for a moment. "And just how do you know this?"

"The lawyer told me. When he was going over the will, he told me that if I ever ran out of money or needed more than what Aunt Ruth left me, that I was to come up here and dig up the treasure. I was told it would be deep and the hole needed to be big in order to find it all."

A gleaming twinkle seemed to light up in Rick's eyes. "See, I knew there was a treasure here somewhere."

Carly watched as an hour went by, then another hour. The hole Rick was digging was now about six feet deep and four feet wide. Oddly enough, she thought, it looked like a grave.

Rick was obviously getting tired. In the moonlight, she could see sweat running down his face and the sound of him panting was the only noise to be heard.

Finally, he threw the shovel up out of the hole onto the ground and using his arms, pulled himself up out after it.

"I do believe you lied to me, Carly," he said, wiping his arm across his forehead to remove the sweat. "There's nothing here."

He took a menacing step toward her. Carly cringed back against the headstone, waiting for the blow that was sure to come.

Suddenly the whole area around them lit up in an otherworldly glow.

Trinny appeared in the space between Carly and Rick.

Rick was able to see her this time.

Trinny's eyes were blackened over and her lips were curled back in a snarl. Her long hair hung down over her face and down her shoulders. She raised her arms out in front of her with her hands curled into claws as she advanced toward him.

Rick's eyes got as big as saucers as Trinny moved closer to him. He lifted up his arms and wrapped them around his face. "NO!" he said. "You're dead! You're not real!" he shouted.

He took a step backward when suddenly the shovel that he had thrown onto the ground was lifted up and swung through the air, connecting with the back of his head. He swung around and stepped to the edge of the hole he had just dug. The ground underfoot gave way and he lost his footing.

Carly watched in slow motion as Rick stumbled and fell backward into the hole he had just dug. A loud thump let her know he had hit the bottom.

Waiting to see if Rick came back up out of the hole, Carly looked to see who had been holding the shovel.

Vernon stood there with the shovel still in his hands. One end in his left fist, the other balanced on his cast. "I don't think he'll be out long. I wasn't able to hit him too hard due to my arm."

Carly stared at him unable to say a word. Everything had happened so fast, she was having a hard time sorting it all out in her mind.

Trinny glided over to Vernon and leaned her face close to his and placed a kiss on his cheek. Carly could have sworn Vernon blushed.

"How did you know we were up here?" Carly asked him.

"Trinny told me," Vernon said. "She came to me this evening and told me you were in trouble. She told me she was leading you to the cemetery and that you needed my help. I saw you and Rick pass by the carriage house. I called the police and told them that something was going on in the cemetery and they needed to get over here. While I was waiting for them, I was wondering what I could do to help when I saw Rick come back down the hill for the shovel. When he passed by again, I followed him. I waited for my chance and when he started toward you, I ran up behind him and grabbed the shovel. It was the only thing I could think do to."

Tears ran down Carly's cheek. "Oh Vernon," she cried. "Thank you so much. Are you ok? You're arm?"

Vernon looked down at his cast. "Oh sure, I'm fine. Knocking that guy out was worth any pain I might have felt."

Carly looked around for Trinny, but she was gone.

"I wouldn't have made it without Trinny," Carly said. "She saved my life. And you, too, of course."

Vernon pulled a pocket knife out of his back pocket and began sawing away on the ropes that bound Carly's hands and feet.

Once she was free, she staggered to her feet and embraced Vernon in a tight hug. "Thank you so much to both you and Trinny."

Vernon patted her back and nodded. "Alright, that's enough of all that mushy stuff. I'm just glad you're alive and unhurt."

Sirens could be heard wailing as they came down the road and turned into the property. Within moments, the cemetery was swarming with police officers.

Rick was still unconscious when the police arrived. They hauled him up out of the hole and slapped him in cuffs and left him laying on the ground while they took statements from Carly and Vernon.

Carly never mentioned seeing Trinny or the role she played in luring Rick out. Who would have believed her anyway?

```
```

Joe was taken to the hospital and treated for a severe concussion and multiple lacerations. Carly felt bad for him. She had accused him of being her intruder and was really rude to him the last time they had talked.

She found out later when she visited him in the hospital that he had been on his way to her place to apologize to her when he stumbled across Rick out in the cemetery. He didn't remember anything that happened after that. The blows to his head had made sure of that.

Trinny's body was exhumed from the tunnel and taken to the coroner's office for examination. Her body was to be released to Carly for burial once the case was closed.

Rick was sent to jail to await a trial. He was charged with the murder of Trinny, the attempted murder of Carly and Joe, breaking and entering and theft. There was enough evidence to put him away for a long time.

Carly's heart was hurt, but she knew, in time, she would move on and get over it. She was disappointed that neither Joe, nor Rick, ended up being her one and only love, but she figured she was still young and the right man would eventually show up. What did Madam Hornbeck know anyway? Follow your heart, she had said. Right...

Carly and Vernon's relationship continued to grow. He remained the grumpy, old man he always was, but Carly learned to love that about him. She returned the love letters she had found in the attic to him. She never opened the rest of them, but slid the one she had read back into the stack and secured a new ribbon around the bundle. Vernon wrapped the silver heart necklace around them and placed the letters alongside the urn in his closet for safe keeping.

Trinny hadn't been seen around the plantation since the night her body had been found. Carly assumed that since her reason for being there had been satisfied, she didn't need to keep coming around. She was going to miss seeing her now that she had gotten past the fear of her, but knew it was probably for the best.

Even with all that had happened, Carly decided to stay at Montgomery Manor and make it her home. There was just something about the old place that drew her to it. She had grown to love it here. It was the only place she could actually call home.

Epilogue

Carly stood next to Vernon in the cemetery at the spot where Trinny was to be laid to rest while the young pastor read from Psalms 23.

It had been several months since Trinny's body had been found and Rick was charged with her murder.

Carly looked at the grave marker she had picked out to sit at the head of Trinny's grave.

The stone angel with her arms outstretched felt appropriate. If it hadn't been for Trinny watching over her, and ultimately helping her, she might not be here today.

Carly looked up from the spot on the ground she had been staring at and saw Trinny's beautiful, ethereal form standing next to Rutherford Montgomery's gravestone.

As she watched, Trinny smiled at her and then transformed before her eyes. Her pale, white skin took on a golden glow. Her eyes were no longer sunk back in her head, but rather shone with a light that reflected love. Her long, dark hair was full and flowing down her back. Her tattered, torn nightgown was replaced with a long, white, flowing gown tied around her waist with a pale pink ribbon. She was simply stunning.

Carly watched, amazed, as a bright light began to form behind Trinny. The light got bigger and brighter until it seemed to wrap around her, completely covering her.

Trinny turned her head toward the light. Looking back at Carly, she nodded and gave her a brilliant smile. Carly smiled back just as Trinny was enveloped into the dazzling light. The light got brighter for a moment, then in a split second, it was gone.

Carly knew that Trinny was finally at peace. She was going to miss seeing her around the place, but was glad that she could finally move on.

Vernon squeezed Carly's hand. When she glanced over at him, he smiled and nodded.

So, he had seen Trinny's transformation and passing over, too. Carly was glad she could share the experience with Vernon.

Smiling to herself, she turned her attention back to the handsome, young pastor.

She had never dated a pastor before. Hhhmmm, maybe she should consider it. She sent up a little prayer asking that maybe, he would be the right man for her.

About the Author

Carol Hall is an American writer who grew up in Chester, West Virginia, but now lives in the mountains of Tennessee.

Carol was inspired to write by her father who loved to tell tall tales to her and her two sisters, as well as to his grandchildren.

Carol's hobbies are reading, hiking, exploring new places and spending time with her family and friends and her three cats.

For more information or to contact Carol, please write to her at,

khiris@att.net

Other Books by Carol Hall

DISAPPEARED- Maggie Stewart loves hiking. Along with her husband and two friends, they set out on a hiking/camping trip in the mountains. Things quickly turn bad as Maggie is kidnapped off the trail by Bigfoot. Now she must fight to survive and try to escape her captors. Will she make it out or be forever lost in the mountains?

THE JOURNEY NORTH- Thirteen year old Emily Dunn is kidnapped from her home in the North and taken to the South to be sold as a slave. The year is 1864. Along the way she meets Mercy and the two become fast friends. One night, they escape their captors and their journey begins as they try to make it back to the North. Along the way they meet some new friends, but are also pursued by their captors. Will they ever make it back home?